"What part of New York are you from?" Scott suddenly asked Mark.

Mark blinked. "What do you mean?"

"It's a simple question, isn't it?" Scott asked. "You've got the accent. I recognize it. So, what part of New York are you from?"

"The Bronx. How about you?"

"Jersey," Scott said.

"Where in Jersey?"

Scott hesitated just a moment. "Galesburg," he said.

"I never heard of it."

"It's there," Scott said, and concentrated on his apple.

As Scott began to demolish the apple, I studied him. *He's lying,* I thought in surprise. *I can see it in his eyes. Why is he lying?*

Don't Scream

Don't Scream

Joan Lowery Nixon

LAUREL-LEAF BOOKS

Published by
Dell Laurel-Leaf
an imprint of
Random House Children's Books
a division of Random House, Inc.
1540 Broadway
New York, New York 10036

Visit us on the Web! www.randomhouse.com/teens

**Educators and librarians, for a variety of teaching tools,
visit us at www.randomhouse.com/teachers**

ISBN: 0-440-22710-0

RL: 5.3

Reprinted by arrangement with Delacorte Press

Printed in the United States of America

October 1997

10 9 8 7 6 5

OPM

For Carol Gorman,
a dear friend

CONFIDENTIAL

FYI ONLY

To: Director Albert P. Harley, Federal Bureau of Investigation, Federal Witness Protection Program

From: Agents Harold Brill and Carl Gless

<u>Notation</u>: Contents of folder to be added to Wayne Arthur Randall file. Last week's newspaper story included.

MOB HEAD CONVICTED

New York: Stavros Grasso, top boss of one of New York City's largest crime organizations, was convicted today on three counts of felony. The damaging eyewitness testimony was given by a member of Grasso's crime ring in a courtroom that had been closed to all unauthorized persons in order to protect the identity of the seventeen-year-old witness.

Two of Grasso's top employees have been arrested as a result of the testimony. The organization's widespread activities in the sale of illegal drugs, forged identifications, prostitution, and . . .

TRANSCRIPT OF SESSION TO OBTAIN JUDICIAL SIGNATURE

COOPER: Wayne Randall . . . I look at you in your neatly pressed suit and realize that to anyone who doesn't know your record, you could easily be mistaken for a model student representing your school.

WAYNE: I *was* a model student, in my own way. School was too easy, if anything.

BRILL: Your Honor, it's just a matter of signing the papers. If you'd . . .

COOPER: Wayne, the psychiatrists who examined you four years ago agreed that you are a sociopath. Do you know what *sociopath* means?

WAYNE: Do I know the big words? I ought to by this time, Your Honor.

2

BRILL: Careful, Wayne.

COOPER: It's the *meaning* of the word I'm concerned with. A sociopath is a person who is antisocial.

WAYNE: [*Laughs*] How about if I change my deodorant?

COOPER: A sociopath can seem open and even charming, which makes him a successful con man. But he's unable to live peaceably with others. He's after self-gratification at the expense of everyone else, because he has no conscience. He doesn't know the meaning of truth. He can be a constant threat . . . a danger to those around him.

BRILL: Not all sociopaths are considered dangerous, Your Honor. There are many who—

COOPER: Don't waste your breath, Mr. Brill. I'm well aware that *all* sociopaths make life difficult for those around them, and those sociopaths with violent histories in childhood will—in most cases—repeat that violence as adults and should be locked up.

BRILL: Your Honor, it's late. If I may say—

COOPER: No, you may *not* say. You have already said your piece—you and the other federal agents who operate your protected witness program. You've made it clear that this is out of my hands. I have no choice but to sign Wayne Randall's release, although it's most decidedly against my wishes and better judgment.

BRILL: Surely Your Honor understands that if Wayne were to retain his own identity, Grasso's crime "family" would retaliate. The least we can do is give Wayne what we've given other protected federal witnesses—a new identity and a new life.

COOPER: What about the lives of others? Wayne Randall has killed before. Without a conscience to stop him, there's every chance in the world he'll murder again.

WAYNE: It wasn't murder, Your Honor. The charge was dropped to manslaughter. I was only thirteen. I was too young to know what I was doing.

COOPER: You knew what you were doing. According to the court records, you robbed the boy, then stabbed him.

WAYNE: That's just part of what happened. I mean, there were so many lies told about me, about how I had planned to stab him. But I hadn't. It was self-defense on my part. And the jury agreed.

COOPER: Self-defense? Do you expect me to believe that? I've dealt with enough sociopaths to know they can be quite disarming and skilled at telling convincing lies. . . . Mr. Brill, from the time Wayne was nine until his last arrest at the age of fifteen, he compiled a long record of arrests for burglary, shoplifting, animal abuse, and—what worries me the most—brutality against other children.

BRILL: *Sealed* records, Your Honor. Records for juvenile offenders are—

COOPER: But we have no record of any arrests during the last two years. Why is that?

BRILL: We—uh—have no actual knowledge that Wayne participated in any criminal activities during this time. He was with and—uh—was . . . he was protected by Grasso's organization.

COOPER: This report mentions an older brother. What about the brother? What type of work does he do for Grasso?

BRILL: Boyd worked as a bodyguard. He was shot and killed six months ago during a drug bust.

COOPER: Let's get this straight, Mr. Brill. In exchange for Wayne's testimony, you're sending him to live in another state. You're giving him a new identity and inflicting him on innocent people who will have no idea that there's a dangerous sociopath in their midst.

BRILL: You're only assuming that he's dangerous. We have the full cooperation of his aunt, who'll be with him. Wayne knows that if he violates the conditions of the Federal Witness Protection Program, he'll be back to square one. We have every hope that his future behavior will—

COOPER: How do his parents fit into all this?

BRILL: They've never been able to deal with either of their sons. They're completely agreeable to the arrangement, Your Honor.

GLESS: If you'll just sign the papers, Your Honor, we'll be on our way.

End of transcript

MEMO:

To Al: Here's the wrap-up. Judge Cooper signed the papers and shoved them at us. Carl and I thanked him and left with Wayne.

It probably means nothing, but just for the record the hallway was empty, except for a male (age and statistics indeterminate) seated on a bench far down the hall.

Neither Carl nor I first paid much attention to him, but we realized, as we left the building, that he had risen to his feet and was walking in our direction. We do not believe he was following us because we didn't see him enter the parking lot. All reasonable security precautions were taken.

Wayne is now established in his new identity and location. Total information is included in enclosed sealed envelope.

Harold

CHAPTER
One

As I plopped down in a shady spot on my front porch steps, cuddling Pepper, my gray-and-white-striped cat, I watched a trio of moving men struggle with the furniture they were delivering to the house next door. They were sweating in the September heat and breathing heavily the pungent odor of salt from Galveston Bay.

I noticed that the furniture was new, but not expensive and not especially good-looking. I was curious. Would these new neighbors be crabby, like old Mr. Chamberlin, who lived at the end of the block? Or maybe young, and have kids?

I sighed. I couldn't help thinking about the kids in the noncontagious children's ward at our county hospital. Little towheaded Ricky had held up his arms to me, begging to be picked up. He'd burrowed his face against my own, making little mewing noises like a kitten. If only . . . But when one end of a pine chest of drawers came down with a crash and the man who had dropped

7

it let out a yell, my attention turned back to the movers.

Last week the For Rent sign had disappeared from the front lawn of the house next door. Yesterday the real estate's cleaning crew had gone through the house. Today was Saturday and my shift at Bingo's Burgers didn't start for another three hours, so I gave way to my curiosity.

A puff of breeze swirled around my shoulders, and I lifted my long, dark hair away from my neck. Darn, it was hot!

An old gray Chevy sedan, which had collected its share of dents, pulled up in front of what had been the Corcoran house, and I watched a middle-aged couple and a guy about my own age climb out. I was shocked—the guy was tall, with broad shoulders, dark brown hair, and a nice face. He wasn't exactly a *ten*, but so close to it that I stood up and deposited Pepper on the step. I sauntered across the dusty grass.

The three newcomers were reaching back inside the car. As they turned, their arms filled with sacks of groceries and an ice chest, I stepped up. "Hi. I'm Jessica Donnally. Welcome to the neighborhood."

Only the guy smiled. The woman, who I assumed was the mother of the family, looked totally stressed out. She glanced at our house and then her own before she nodded at me.

"We're the Maliks. We'll have to get acquainted later. It's been a long drive. Then we wasted hours in that realtor's office. There's so much to do." Her words were rapid and clipped and angry. I had to think a moment before they registered.

Mrs. Malik pushed a strand of dirty blond hair away from her face and walked toward the rented house, her hips straining against a skirt that was a little too heavy and much too tight. Her husband, short and stocky in a rumpled madras shirt and khaki pants, simply followed.

"Don't mind them," the guy said with an unfamiliar accent. "Mom didn't want to move to Texas. She's mad at Dad and at me . . . at the whole world, I guess. She needs time and she'll come around."

He grinned, and it was so contagious I grinned back. "I'm Mark . . . Mark Malik," he said. "You said your name is Jessica?"

"Everyone calls me Jess."

"Hi, Jess. I suppose we'll be going to the same high school."

"Since we've only got one high school—Oakberry High—you're right! Where are you folks from, Mark?"

His smile was warm, but instead of answering, he said, "We'll talk later. You can fill me in on what I'll need to know." He shifted the load in his arms and headed up the walk.

I went back across the grass into my house. Taking the stairs two at a time, then flinging myself across my bed, I snatched up the telephone and dialed my best friend, Lori Roberts. She answered on the second ring.

"Guess what!" I said. "New guy at school. He's cute."

9

"You're right. He is," Lori said. "I saw him registering in Mrs. Shappley's office late this afternoon."

I gave a bounce, and the bed creaked noisily. "You won't believe it! He moved in next door to me."

Lori groaned. "How come you get all the luck?"

"Wait a minute," I said as I suddenly realized what Lori had told me. "You said you saw him registering at school. You couldn't have. He just got here. His mother was complaining about the long drive."

"The guy I saw is blond—hair about the same color as mine—and he's medium tall," Lori said. "By the way, Mrs. Shappley put him in our English lit class."

I shook my head at the phone. "Mark Malik isn't blond. He has dark brown hair. It's almost as dark as mine."

"Two new guys." Lori's smile warmed her voice. "Life is looking up!"

When Mom got home from her job at the bank and Dad walked into the kitchen, damp and sticky from the lessons he gave as a golf pro, I told them about the new neighbors.

Dad gulped down half a glass of cold water, wiped a hand across his mouth, and said, "Frank and Eloise Malik."

"How'd you know?" I asked.

"Elmer Butler told me. He's the one who rented them the house."

"Where are they from?"

"New Jersey, New York, someplace like that," Dad answered. He polished off the water and asked, "Does it make a difference?"

I shrugged. "I just wondered."

Dad smiled as he reached over and tousled my hair. "I swear, Jess, you're as curious as a cat."

"If you're comparing me to cats, leave out Pepper," I told him. "He's not the least bit curious. All he does is eat and sleep."

"Jess," Mom said as she kicked off her shoes, "you peel the potatoes. Phil, why don't you get the grill going outside? I can put together something for our new neighbors."

Mom, her short, dark hair curling damply around her face, changed from her tailored skirt and blouse into shorts and a T-shirt. She decided to bake a Lazy Daisy sheet cake with a caramel-coconut broiled frosting. It's quick, it's easy, and it's Mom's specialty. She's well known for it at church suppers and school bake sales. No one in Oakberry has ever been known to turn down a piece of her cake.

After we'd finished eating supper, she wrapped the still-warm cake pan in a kitchen towel and handed it to me. I was about to leave, already wearing my red-and-white-checked apron and cap —the uniform for my evening shift at Bingo's.

Mom grinned and said, "From what you told me about the Maliks, I suspect that you'd like to deliver this."

I grinned back, at ease with her teasing. Sure, there are problems between us at times, because

11

Mom doesn't just say something, she goes on and on about it, as if I can't figure out things for myself. But sometimes she's great.

"Mark Malik *is* kind of cute, Mom. He's tall. Taller than me. It's not always easy to find really tall dates. Except for Eric, it's almost impossible."

"Eric?"

"You remember Eric Dodson. I picked him out in seventh grade because he was the only boy in my class taller than me."

"Than I."

"Yeah. Taller than you, too." I giggled, then sighed. "Eric has always had possibilities. I even thought I had a chance until he fell in love with a computer. He hasn't been interested in anything else since then."

"When I was your age I had the same trouble finding tall dates," Mom said. "When I went out on dates I wore ballet slippers."

"But you lucked out. You met Dad." I pretended to frown. "All those tall genes. No wonder I ended up five feet ten."

"Look at the bright side," Mom kidded. "Just think—you'll always be able to reach the top shelves." She looked at her watch. "Mrs. Malik isn't going to feel like seeing company right away. Just drop this off on your way to work and tell the Maliks we'll do our neighboring later."

I carefully carried the cake across the lawn and up the steps of the Maliks' porch. As I balanced the flat, rectangular pan on one hand and prepared to ring the doorbell, I heard Mrs. Malik snap, "Don't push your luck."

12

A deeper voice—Mark? Mr. Malik?—said, "Like it or not, we're here. You can spend your time griping, or calm down and make the best of it."

"If it weren't for . . ." Mrs. Malik moved away from the door, and I couldn't catch the rest of what she said.

I knew I couldn't ring the doorbell now. As quietly as I could, I tiptoed down the porch steps, walked a few feet, then turned to face the Maliks' house. Humming loudly, I clumped up the stairs and across the porch.

Mr. Malik opened the door and faced me before I'd had a chance to knock.

"Hi," I said. "Remember me? Jess Donnally. I live next door. My mom sent over this welcome cake. She'll come and visit some other time, after you're settled in."

He took the warm pan, stared at the cake in bewilderment, then managed to say, "Thank you," before shutting the door firmly behind him.

Weird, I thought. *Except for good-looking Mark, that is a truly weird family.*

CHAPTER
two

A short while later, I was busy serving burgers, fries, and Cokes, chatting with the customers, and flashing a friendly Bingo's Burgers smile, when Mark Malik stepped up to the counter.

"Hi. Thanks for bringing over the cake. It was great," he said.

"Mom made it. It's one of her specialties. I'm glad you liked it," I said.

Mark lowered his voice. "I'm afraid my dad wasn't very friendly when you came. He should have invited you in. It's just that the cake kind of took us by surprise."

"Why were you surprised?"

Mark shrugged. "Well, because we weren't expecting anything like that."

"Really? Mom's cake was just the beginning. Mrs. Snyder, across the street, will probably bring over a fresh peach pie, and Mrs. Hickey will show up with a meat loaf. You know the custom. It's called being neighborly."

"That's a custom? I never heard of doing anything like that."

"Well, I never heard of *not* doing it." I paused, aware of the line that was beginning to form behind Mark, but my curiosity won out. "Where did you say you're from?" I asked.

"The East Coast," he answered.

"Where on the East Coast aren't they neighborly?"

Linda Pruett leaned around Mark's shoulder and said, "Jessie, what's keeping this line? I've got four hungry kids waiting to eat. They're going to tear up this place if I don't get some food inside them pretty quick."

"Sorry," Mark said, and he stepped back, giving Mrs. Pruett a glowing smile.

Caught off guard, she patted his arm and said, "That's all right, son. I'm sorry to have to interrupt."

"No problem," Mark said. With a wave in my direction, he strode to Bingo's main door and left.

"Two doubles and four treasure boxes, and no cheese on the burgers," Mrs. Pruett said, quickly collecting herself. "Cokes all around, and make sure none of the treasure boxes are missing their prizes this time." She jerked her chin toward the door. "That was a good-looking boy you were talking to, Jessie. Seems like a nice, polite boy, too. I haven't seen him around here before. Did his family recently move to Oakberry?"

"Yes," I answered as I scrawled the order and

15

clipped it to the trolley leading to the open kitchen. "They moved in today."

"What's their name?"

"Malik."

"Any relation to the Maliks down around Sweet Home or Halletsville?"

"I don't think so." I told Mrs. Pruett the total, took the bills she handed me, and gave her change.

"Where are they from?" Mrs. Pruett persisted.

"The East Coast," I said. "That's all Mark told me." I loaded Mrs. Pruett's order on a large tray and turned to the next customer.

Mark obviously had come to Bingo's just to see me. Hugging a little smile that no one could see, I promised myself that as soon as possible I was going to find out as much as I could about Mark Malik.

It was getting late, near the end of my shift, when Eric Dodson wandered in. He squinted up at the menu board, which spread across the counter area over my head, then looked at me.

"Hi, Jess," he said.

"Hi," I answered. "What'll you have, Eric?"

"Baked potato," he said.

"We don't have baked potatoes," I told him. "Fries okay?"

Eric frowned and studied the menu board again while I studied him. When I was in seventh grade, I thought Eric was really something. He's probably the smartest person I've ever met, and he's good-looking in a skinny-tall kind of way. Eric's father tried all year to get him to go out for basketball,

16

but his grandmother gave him his first computer. No one saw much of Eric after that. From my point of view, it's terrible to see a really tall guy go to waste.

"How about a Meal-in-One?" I suggested. "Double meat patty, two kinds of cheese, lots of tomatoes, lettuce, pickles, and onion. Fries on the side, along with a milk shake. It covers most of your basic food groups."

"Okay," Eric said, and grinned. "What you said was pure advertising hype, but at least I can report back to my mom that I had the basic food groups."

"Anything to make your mom happy," I said. I took his money, wrote down his order, and clipped it to the trolley.

Eric rolled his eyes. "Happy? It's very hard to make her happy." No one was at the counter, so he leaned toward me. "My mom gets uptight about things, like my showing up tonight for dinner. She kept yelling upstairs for me to come down, and I kept telling her I couldn't come right then. I was in a chat group with some very interesting Latin professors, who were discussing the demise of classical languages, and I felt I should explain to them that Latin wasn't totally dead in high-school curricula. Well, anyway, when the discussion was over, I came down to the kitchen to see if anything was left or get a couple of Pop-Tarts to take back upstairs, and that made her even more upset. That's why I'm here."

"Welcome to Bingo's Burgers," I said, and handed him his order.

17

"The older generation just can't seem to adapt to modern technology," Eric said.

I just smiled and realized I wasn't going to worry about tall, dateless Eric. I had my mind on Mark Malik.

ON SUNDAY, AFTER services at Oakberry Baptist Church, Lori came over. She and I—"the long and the short of it," as Dad liked to tease—decided to hang out on the front porch, hoping that Mark would emerge from his house and come over. But there was no sign of any of the Maliks.

"Their car's on the driveway, so they must be home," Lori said.

I picked up sleepy old Pepper and draped him over my shoulder, snuggling my chin against his soft, warm back. A bee burrowed into a golden, out-of-season blossom on the Confederate jasmine, and a half-dozen grackles swooped down on the front yard, searching the grass for bugs. "It's probably the September heat," I told Lori. "It takes people from the East a while to get used to Texas weather. They don't want to go outside and leave their air-conditioning."

Lori nodded and stretched. "Well, if you think Wonder Boy isn't coming out so I can get a good look at him, why don't we walk through the woods over to the bay? And don't tell me it's too far out of the way to go through the woods, because it's a lot cooler."

I stood up. "No argument," I said. "I don't have to go to work until four."

The woods—which had never been given a proper name—was a scraggly patch of pine, tallow, and oak—an unlovely offshoot trailing down from the thick swath of forest that spread northward and outward from Houston, through the northeastern counties of Texas, into Arkansas and Louisiana. But the outskirts of the woods—the only part I was allowed in—were one of my favorite places. Cool and quiet, with a thick padding of damp, spongy mulch underfoot, it was a solitary place in which to think and dream.

When I was little, I'd often heard the rumor that deep inside the woods were the remains of an ancient cemetery.

"Early settlers," Mrs. Snyder had explained. "I doubt if folks even remember where the cemetery is now. Long ago the trees grew up and hid the graves. Something nasty is attached to that place. It's best left forgotten."

Mrs. Hickey's smile had been smug. "It wasn't settlers who got buried there. From what I've heard, it's Harry Pratt's last resting place."

"Who's Harry Pratt?" I'd asked, and Mom had suddenly noticed me.

"Harry Pratt was one of the meanest train robbers in these parts, that's who," Mrs. Hickey had said.

"Pishtosh," Mrs. Snyder had answered. "There've never been any trains around here to rob."

"Why don't we talk about the PTA spaghetti supper," Mom began, one eye on me.

Mrs. Hickey wasn't finished. "Harry Pratt had

19

family here," she announced. "I understand he was related to the William Pratt family, who long ago moved down Houston way."

"Pishtosh," Mrs. Snyder repeated.

The minute our guests had gone, Mom sat down opposite me, her face close to mine, and said, "I know you've got an active imagination, Jessie love, but don't waste time getting scared over those silly stories about a cemetery. People like to talk about one being back there, hidden in the woods, but far as I know, no one's ever seen it."

"I'm not scared," I answered honestly. I'd seen the Oakberry cemetery, with its ornate head-stones, American flags, and fat bunches of faded artificial flowers; I tried to imagine what a secret, hidden cemetery would look like. Might there be a stone angel with outstretched wings? Or were train robbers not allowed to have angels? Someday I'd take a look for myself and find out if Harry Pratt was really buried there.

"Put your right hand over your heart, Jessie," Mom had demanded, "and promise me you won't go looking for that cemetery. Not now when you're a little girl and not when you're older. *Not ever.*"

"Why?" I asked, but Mom's gaze grew stern.

"Because it's not a safe place."

"Why not?"

"Jessica Donnally!" Mom snapped in an explosive tone that meant business. "You're not to go because I said so. That's why."

20

Of course I was forever curious about the cemetery, but a promise was a promise. I'd kept my word.

As Lori and I ambled through the outskirts of the woods, breathing in the earthy, sour-sweet smells that rose from the ground under our feet, Lori said, "I've never seen anyone here but us. There's nothing in these woods worth hunting, and no shortcuts to anyplace through here."

"As you pointed out," I said, "it even takes longer for us to get to the bay if we take this route. We only do it because we like to."

Ahead of us lay a cluster of boulders we'd named Castle Rock, which marked a turning point in the route toward the bay. I sprinted ahead and scrambled up the boulders until I reached the top. "Remember when we were kids and first named this our castle?" I called down to Lori. "We made up a whole routine of punches and kicks that we'd use on anybody who tried to take over our castle." I laughed. "I still remember the routine. Hard fist to the stomach first, which makes the bad guy go *ooof!* and bend over. Then we make a double fist with both hands and bring it up under his chin, which causes him to bend backward."

"Don't forget the *ooof!*" Lori said.

"Right. Another *ooof!* We follow with another jab to the stomach, and when he falls forward we end with a neck chop."

I sighed. "Lori, I need to talk to you."

She pulled herself up to the top boulder and squeezed next to me. "What's the problem?"

"Remember when our social problems class took a field trip through the Community Hospital's children's ward, with all those little kids?"

"Sure, I remember. Why?"

"They have an awfully small staff of nurses."

"What are you talking about?" Lori asked.

"About the kids. Some of them are real little, and they need people to play with them and hold them. A lot of them are charity cases, and sometimes their parents aren't able to visit them more than a couple of times a month. Remember Ricky —the little boy who's in the middle of a series of operations?"

When Lori nodded, I continued, "The director told us that because Ricky spends most of his waking hours in his crib he can't walk yet. Thirteen months old, and there's no one who has the time to help him learn to walk!"

"Are you worried about the kids? Is that it?"

I shifted position and rubbed my right leg, which was beginning to prickle. "That's what I want to talk to you about. What if we get some of the kids at school together to volunteer to spend a few hours each afternoon and on the weekend to play with the kids? We could each pick a day."

"What day?" Lori looked pained. "Besides school and homework, I've got piano lessons, choir practice, and driver's ed. And look at you— Saturday and Sunday afternoons you work at Bingo's."

I turned so abruptly I had to grab Lori, who nearly slid off the rock. "But you're almost through with driver's ed, so you could volunteer for Wednesdays. And I'm . . ." I sank back, taking a deep breath. "Maybe I should quit my job at Bingo's, or at least cut back the hours. I can't stop thinking about those little kids, Lori—especially Ricky—and the way they need us. Nothing else seems as important. I feel so selfish sometimes. Do you know what I mean?"

"Sure I do. But what about your mom and dad? Have you told them you want to quit your job?"

"I haven't told anyone but you," I said, and squirmed uncomfortably. I wished Lori hadn't brought up my parents.

"I mean you're supposed to be helping to save money toward college expenses."

"I know that."

"And my dad says it costs more and more. Rice, for instance . . ."

I hugged my knees. "Oh, come on, Lori. I get good enough grades, but I have as much chance of Rice's accepting me as Harvard or Yale. If I go to the College of the Mainland or one of the junior colleges, it will cost a lot less. I can handle it."

"I think you should talk to your parents."

"I will." I turned to face her. "You don't know how much I want to do this. I didn't even know until I started talking about it to you. It means a lot to me. Will you help me see if we can get some volunteers and do something to help these kids?"

"I think you ought to talk to Mrs. Emery, too, and see what she thinks. I mean before you quit your job or anything drastic like that," Lori said.

"I'd thought about that," I told her.

"Speaking of Mrs. Emery," Lori said, "I've got

an idea for that term paper she wants on neighbor-hood relations, but I don't know if it really fits. Our next-door neighbor is such a pill. And look at your neighborhood. I mean, how can you have good relations with a crab like Mr. Chamberlin, who yells at everybody to get off his lawn?"

"Mom and Dad have good relations with him," I said. "He's just a bitter old man to feel sorry for."

Lori sighed. "I know. Your mother sends him cakes and things, and your dad even installed one of those safety lights on his front porch. Has he ever pushed the button to blink on and off and made your dad come running?"

"No," I said. "Even that old Persian cat of his is crabby!"

"Peaches!" Lori said. "What a name for an ugly yellow cat! She looks just like Mr. Chamberlin, if you think about it, and the way he acts about her . . ."

As Lori went on, a creepy feeling spread over me. I found myself glancing again and again into the groves of trees, dim shadows that were splotched with narrow patches of light. Lori and I were alone. There was no sign of another human being, yet my back prickled as though someone was staring at us. The prickly feeling wouldn't go away.

"Let's go back," I whispered to Lori.

"I thought we were going to walk to the bay. Then you wanted to climb up here to talk and—"

"I think we should go home instead."

"What's the matter with you, Jess?"

"I don't know," I whispered. "I have the feeling that someone's here in the woods with us."

Lori's head swiveled. "Where?"

"There's no telling. I don't see anybody. But I feel someone looking at us. Don't you?"

Lori's eyes widened, and she wiggled closer. "You're scaring me, Jess."

"Then climb down. We'll go home." I led the way.

Lori scurried down the rocks and dropped to the ground beside me. Her voice was breathy with fear. "Now you've got me doing it. I feel it, too. But why would anybody hide and stare at us?"

"I don't know, but it's weird. Let's go."

As we turned to retrace our steps, Lori asked, "What if whoever it is comes after us?"

"Run!" I cried, but Lori was already ahead of me.

CHAPTER
three

Lori and I raced to my house, where we sat on the porch steps while catching our breath.

"Maybe it was our imagination," Lori was finally able to say. She looked at me accusingly. "Or yours. No one followed us."

I sat up and brushed my hair out of my face. "But didn't you feel that someone was there?"

Lori shrugged. "It might have been some kids playing pranks. Or it could have been Mr. Chamberlin. Maybe he bent down to tie a shoe, and that's why we didn't see him."

"Oh, come on, Lori. Mr. Chamberlin wouldn't walk in the woods. He uses a cane, and he's afraid of falling down. Besides, we would have seen Peaches. She's always with him."

Pepper emerged from a shadowy corner of the porch, stretched lazily, and climbed into my lap. I stroked him and said, "We should have had Pepper with us. Cats can see things that humans can't."

Lori shivered. "Don't do that. If somebody's hiding just to spy on us, I don't want to see him."

"Not even to find out who he is?"

"Not even then." Lori made a face. "Honestly, Jess, you've got to know everything!"

I smiled. "It makes life interesting."

The front door opened, and Mom strode out. She plopped down on the top step. "I can't believe it!" she exploded.

"Believe what?" I asked. "What are you so steamed about?"

Mom drew in a long breath and blew it out slowly. "I have no right to be upset," she said. "I'm just surprised, that's all."

"About what?"

"The cake I sent to our new neighbors. Well, I found the empty, washed cake pan at our back door. Almost stumbled over it. And not even a note of thanks with the pan. I don't know what to make of it."

"Mark told me they were surprised when you sent over the cake," I explained. "People on the East Coast don't send over stuff to new neighbors."

"Nonsense," Mom said. "Taking over food to help people settle in is the way people try to be neighborly everywhere, not just in Texas. And don't say *stuff*. My cake was a *cake*, not *stuff*."

I glanced in the direction of the Maliks' house. "I just noticed. Their car's gone," I said to Lori.

Mom looked at us as though suddenly seeing us

for the first time and said, "Surely you girls weren't running in this heat, were you?"

"We were in the woods," I said. "It's cooler there."

Mom stood and shook her head. "The follies of the young," she said. "Just don't overdo it and come down with heat exhaustion."

"Okay, I promise. We won't." As soon as the front door closed behind her, I turned to Lori. "No one besides us ever goes into the woods, but Mark's new here. What if he went exploring?"

Lori looked puzzled. "If he *was* in the woods and he saw us, he'd come over and say hello, wouldn't he?"

"I guess so. He should."

"Well, of course he should. Anyway, we sat out here forever, and we didn't see him leave his house."

"Hey, look!" Lori whispered, jabbing me in the ribs. "The Maliks' car?"

I watched as the car came to a stop at the curb and Mark climbed out—alone. He smiled at me and strode toward us.

"Yum! Nice smile!" Lori murmured under her breath.

"Hi," Mark said to me before he turned to Lori.

"Lori Roberts, this is Mark Malik—our new next-door neighbor," I said.

"Hi, Lori," Mark said. "Shall I put you down for brownies?"

He laughed at the puzzled look on Lori's face.

"Jess told me that around here everyone brings the new neighbors something to eat. I just thought I'd make a pitch for brownies while I had the chance."

"Sit down," I said. "No brownies on hand, but I can get some Cokes."

"No thanks. Some other time," Mark answered. "I've got work to do. I just came back from the hardware store. I bought what I need to put up shelves."

The front door opened, and Mom walked onto the porch. "You must be Mark Malik," she said. "Jess has told me about you."

As Mark jumped up the lower steps to shake Mom's hand, I scooted aside to make room, but Pepper leaped out of the way and ran around the corner of the house.

Mark laughed. "Your cat left in a big hurry. Was it something I said?"

"Don't mind Pepper," I answered. "There's no telling what got into him."

Mark looked up at Mom and said, "I'm glad to meet you, Mrs. Donnally. Thanks for the cake. It was great."

"Please thank your mother for returning the pan," Mom answered. "I'm disappointed that I didn't get to meet her."

I could hear the trace of coolness in Mom's voice, but Mark didn't seem to notice.

"She's eager to meet you, too, and to thank you for being so kind," Mark said, "but my dad's under the weather, and my mom's kind of worried about him. Ever since his heart attack . . ." He stopped and smiled at Mom. "My mother wants to ask you how you made that terrific frosting with the coconut and—was it *brown* sugar?"

While Mom, totally won over, recited the recipe and asked Mark about his father's health, I stared at his shoes, planted so close to where I was sitting. They were an expensive dark gray suede—not right for Texas weather at all—and clinging to their rough, damp-stained surface were what looked like bits of leaf mold . . . the kind found in forests, not in shopping malls.

Don't be so suspicious, I cautioned myself. *Mark cut across the grass when he saw us. That's just grass on his shoes.*

"So please tell your mother I'm planning to come calling as soon as she's had time to settle in," Mom said.

"I will," Mark said. "Glad to meet you, Lori. See you later, Jess."

He jogged down the steps and to his car, removed two large paper bags from the trunk, and carried them into his house.

"What a lovely boy," Mom said. "There's something different about him. He's so polite . . . so . . . I guess I'd say *charming*. That's it. He's charming."

As she went inside the house, Lori murmured, "Who cares about charming? He's a hunk."

"He sure is," I said. My misgivings vanished with Lori's giggles.

* * *

THE NEXT MORNING Mark rang my doorbell. "I wish I could offer you a ride to school," he said, "but I haven't got a car of my own yet. My mom and dad have to use the car to get to work."

"It's a short walk," I told him, glad that he had put away his Eastern clothing and dressed for the heat in a T-shirt and jeans. I grabbed my backpack, yelled goodbye to my parents, and headed for the sidewalk with Mark.

"Where do your parents work?" I asked.

"They're both with the MaxiMart chain," he said.

"Oh. Then they were transferred here. Right?"

"Right."

We came to Mr. Chamberlin's house, next to the Maliks', and Mark started to cut across Mr. Chamberlin's lawn to round the corner.

"Wait," I said. I put a hand on his arm and tugged him back to the sidewalk.

Mark looked surprised. "What's wrong with the shortcut?"

"Mr. Chamberlin's old and kind of crabby. He doesn't want anyone walking on his grass."

"Should we care what the old guy wants?" Mark took a step in the direction of Mr. Chamberlin's velvet-green lawn.

"I care," I said, and tugged him along, down the sidewalk.

Mark followed reluctantly, but as we came to the thick, neatly trimmed bushes of pink oleander that decorated the corner of Mr. Chamberlin's lot, Mark grabbed a fistful of branches and shook them.

31

A loud screech made us both jump.

As Peaches streaked across the lawn toward the safety of her house, I said, "Run! Before he comes out and yells at us!"

We were around the corner, out of sight, before we heard Mr. Chamberlin's screen door fly open. "Who's out there?" he yelled. "What cowardly, stupid oaf is trying to harm my cat?"

When we stopped for breath, Mark and I both laughed.

"You've learned something about Oakberry already," I told Mark. "To keep from getting your head chewed off, you have to stay clear of Mr. Chamberlin and his cat."

"What makes him so mean?" Mark asked.

"I don't think he even knows he's mean," I said. "He used to be okay. About fifteen years ago his wife and two daughters were killed by a drunk driver who got off the charges. Mr. Chamberlin can't get over it. Mom said he shriveled up like a mealy old apple left in the sun. He's never stopped grieving. He only has his cat left. I kind of feel sorry for him."

Mark chuckled as he tapped my arm with his fist. "You would," he teased.

As we continued our walk to school, I said, "You were telling me about your parents. Which MaxiMart do they work in? The nearest one in Gulfgate Mall?"

"Yes, but why are we talking about my parents?" Mark asked. "You said you'd fill me in, so tell me what I should know about school and what I should watch out for."

I almost tripped over a tree root that had broken through the sidewalk, just managing to catch my balance. "What do you mean 'watch out for'? What are you talking about?"

"School politics. Teachers to avoid. Gangs. Whatever."

I smiled. "There aren't any gangs in Oakberry. We're too small a town for gangs."

"You've got to have some people hanging out together. If you don't call them gangs, then what do you call them?"

I looked at Mark, but he kept his gaze straight ahead. "Friends," I said evenly.

Mark stared at me questioningly, doubt in his eyes.

"I'm not kidding," I said. "The jocks and their girlfriends hang out together, the computer fiends spend their lunch hours off somewhere on the Internet, the most popular kids—"

"Most popular. That's where you fit in. Right?"

There was something about his tone of voice, something about the way he asked the question that I didn't like. I shifted my backpack and began to walk faster. "No. They're the rich kids whose parents have big homes down on the bay. Sorry to disappoint you."

Mark didn't speak as he kept pace beside me. Then suddenly he put an arm around my shoulders. His voice was light and warm as he said, "Wherever you are, Jess, that's a good place to be."

My face grew warm. *Take it easy*, I cautioned

myself. *He's coming on awfully fast. Mark may turn out to be the nicest guy I've ever met, or . . .*

"It's hard to come into a new school in your junior year," Mark said. "I need a friend to help me through the worst of it. I can't afford to make any mistakes that might land me in trouble."

Amazed, I turned and stared at him. "Why should you get in trouble? I don't understand."

He dropped his arm from my shoulders and took a step away. "I'll be honest with you," he said. "I've got a temper. Sometimes I blow up when I shouldn't."

He turned on the full power of his smile, and I felt the charge right down to my toes. "Stick with me, Jess," he said. "Help me stay in line. Okay?"

What had Mom said about Mark? Polite and charming. That was it. So why was I looking for something that wasn't there?

Flustered, I tried to keep things easy. "Which am I—a guiding star or a shining light?" I asked.

"Both," he said, and we laughed.

We turned a corner, and I pointed out the boxy, two-story, orange-red brick building at the end of the next block. "There's Oakberry High," I said.

Mark looked at his watch and shrugged. "Before we get there you've got time to tell me something about yourself. You're interested in more than school and homework and serving burgers and fries. What's on your mind, Jess? What do you want to do with yourself?"

I stammered, "C-College after graduation next year. Maybe social work, helping kids."

34

"And?"

"What do you mean?"

"I mean, what else? You've got a life *now*."

I shrugged. "Now I've got an idea, but I need to tell my mom and dad what I want to do and then let Mrs. Emery in on it."

"Mrs. Emery?"

"She teaches our class in social problems. She's the one who set up a field trip to visit local caregiving agencies."

He looked puzzled, so I explained, "Welfare agency, crisis hot line, child-abuse prevention center, and the children's ward at our county's Community Hospital."

"Let me guess," Mark said. "They all need help. That's what you're thinking of. Right?"

For a moment my mouth fell open. When I could talk, I asked, "How could you know that?"

"Easy," he said. "Now it's just a matter of figuring out which agency you're interested in and what you want to do." He smiled and said, "They probably all have fund-raising social events, and high-school students aren't usually at the top of the guest list, so fund-raising isn't your goal. Hmmm. Whatever you have in mind means volunteer work. Am I right again?"

"Yes," I said.

He continued to study my face. "And the volunteer work involves kids."

"Okay," I said. My laugh was a little shaky. "I don't know how you do it, but you ought to take your mind-reading act on the road."

It was Mark's turn to laugh. "I did it by watch-

35

ing your face. When I mentioned kids you kind of lit up. You gave yourself away. You're easy to figure out, Jess."

"Are you always this good at reading people?"

"Wait! I'm not through," he said. "Whatever plan you've got in mind probably involves other volunteers, too."

"What!"

"Well, if it was just something you wanted to do yourself, you wouldn't have to talk to your social problems teacher and make such a big deal of it."

"Listen, Mark," I said. "I do have a plan in mind to help out with the little kids in the hospital's children's ward, but I don't want to talk about it yet. I haven't worked it all out, and Lori reminded me I should talk to my parents first . . . I mean about my job at Bingo's and my other responsibilities."

"Lori believes that you should never walk into a new situation unless you're covered."

"Covered?"

"You know . . . like having all the bases covered." Mark's smile was easy. "It's a good idea and a good move. You'll make points as a model citizen."

"That's not why I—"

"Take it easy," he said. "I know that's not why. I was just teasing."

As we reached the main building, I left Mark to make his way through the enrollment paperwork and met Lori in our usual spot, under the large oak tree next to the gym.

36

Lori gave a little hop. "I talked to him this morning!" she squealed. "He's in our first class, and he is real cute—sort of brooding and mysterious."

I smiled. "That's straight out of *Wuthering Heights*. Remember? We read it last year. Does this brooding, mysterious man stalk over the moors, too?"

"Very funny," Lori said. She tried to sound indignant, but she giggled. "Wait until you meet Scott. You'll see what I mean."

As the first bell rang, we entered the main building and walked toward our lockers.

"His name is Scott Alexander," Lori volunteered.

"Nice name," I said, "but it doesn't fit somebody who's brooding on the moors."

I dumped my backpack inside my locker, took only my English lit book and notebook, and walked to class, greeting most of the kids. In a town the size of Oakberry, there weren't many people I didn't know.

As I slid into my desk, near the back of the room, Lori nudged me and nodded toward a long-legged guy in the last seat of the window row. He was tall and a little too thin, and his high cheekbones looked as though they'd been molded by someone with an artist's touch. A shock of his thick blond hair fell back from his forehead as he raised deep blue eyes to Lori.

He didn't smile. He merely nodded recognition, but Lori glowed as she quickly introduced us and asked Scott a question.

37

I didn't hear either the question or the answer. I was captivated by the intensity of Scott's eyes, which completely hid whatever thoughts lay behind them.

CHAPTER
four

Mark didn't show up until our third-period social problems class. As he slid into the chair next to me, his eyes glittered with anger, and his breath came in hard, quick spurts.

"What happened?" I asked.

"The papers should have been in order, but they weren't." Mark spat out the words. "No math listed. Stupid dorks! And that warden downstairs in the office—she acts like her whole life depends on having the right forms filled out."

"I'm sorry," I said. I found myself nervously drawing back from the raging fire that possessed him.

Mark turned from me, rested his chin on his chest, closed his eyes, and took three long, deep breaths. When he looked back, I could sense that he had recognized my fear.

Why blame me? I thought, positive that I wasn't the only person who wanted to get out of the way when Mark turned angry.

"I have better things to do than sit in an office

for two hours," Mark said, and to my surprise his voice was now steady, with a hint of humor in it. "The clerk downstairs wouldn't take my word that I'd had Algebra Two. She had to try to reach my mom, who called back from work, and now Mom has to call my former school to get them to correct my records so I can be admitted. They finally allowed me to come to class when I told the clerk, 'Forget the whole thing. I'm walking out.' "

"They'll fix the records," I said. "It's no big problem." I was puzzled because Mark had made it a bigger deal than the situation warranted. He'd confided he had a temper, and it was obviously true.

Lori and Scott were the last to come into the classroom, slipping into two seats in the window row just as Mrs. Emery began taking roll, glancing back and forth from her students to her list, soundlessly mouthing their names.

"Scott Alexander and Mark Malik," she finally said. "Welcome to our class. Which of you is Scott, and which is Mark?"

Each identified himself, and Mrs. Emery said, "You'll have a lot of catching up to do. The text is just part of what you learn here. We try to approach community problems in an original, positive manner. Active participation in class discussions is not only encouraged, it's expected. Today you'll discover what we do in class. After that, if you have any questions . . ."

Mark raised his hand, but even before Mrs. Emery could respond, he spoke up. "If you're looking

40

for action and not just talk, Jess—Jessica Donnally—and I have been discussing the biggest need at the Community Hospital's children's ward, which is volunteers, and the ways that the people in this class could help."

What is Mark doing? In shock I gripped the edge of the desk so hard my fingers hurt. "Not yet, Mark!" I blurted out. "I mean, I'd rather discuss this idea when it's all worked out, Mrs. Emery."

Mrs. Emery sat on the edge of her desk and smiled. "Why wait? I'd like to hear what you and Mark have in mind, Jessica. It might be a project the entire class can do together. Why don't you or Mark stand up and tell us about it?"

Reluctantly I slid out of my chair and faced the group. I knew my face was burning. I wanted to hold my hands to my cheeks, hiding behind them, but I said, "Last week, when we visited the children's ward, it was obvious that the staff is so small that the kids badly needed more attention—people to play with them or to read to them. A little boy named Ricky stays mostly in his crib because no one has the time to teach him to walk. The head nurse said that his mother had to work two jobs and wasn't able to visit him often. And I—"

Suddenly Mark was beside me, his hand pressing my shoulder. "Jess and I talked about setting up a regular volunteer program," he said. "High-school kids could help out every afternoon after class and even on weekends. People could sign up for whatever times they had open."

Mark went on to describe how great it would

feel to read to a kid who might never have heard a story or to teach a child to catch a ball. The pressure of his hand increased, and I found myself sinking into my chair.

A finger poked the middle of my back, and I turned to see Lori stretching toward me. "Did you talk to your parents already?" she whispered.

I shook my head, and her eyes widened in surprise. "Then why . . . ?"

Shrugging, I turned back to face Mrs. Emery, who gleamed as though someone had turned on her power switch.

"This is a good idea, and it's completely workable," she said. "It gives a teacher hope that all those days spent in the classroom with kids who 'didn't know we had any homework' can turn out to be worthwhile."

Suddenly Scott spoke up. "We should form an organizing committee," he said. "I'd like to be on it."

"So far we're just talking about it," Mark said, and turned and stared at Scott.

"Just talking won't get us anywhere," Scott said challengingly.

Mark's voice was tight. "We can set up a committee when we're ready," he began, but Mrs. Emery stepped in.

"Setting up a committee is a good idea. I don't know how much of this project is Jessica's idea and how much is Mark's, but I'd suggest that Jessica head the committee because of her familiarity with Oakberry."

"Actually, I—I've got to talk to my parents and

42

see if I can make some changes in my job hours," I stammered.

Mark interrupted. "Jess is the brains behind all this," he said, "but the job of committee chair means that someone's going to have to supervise, to make sure all the volunteers show up when they're supposed to, and even to take the places of the volunteers who find out at the last minute that they won't be able to come. Maybe being new here is an advantage, because I've got lots of free time. I'll be glad to be the committee chair."

"Jess should head the committee," Scott insisted. "She won't have to quit her job to do it. She can handle the work if we help her."

Mark's glance was cold as it flicked from Scott to me, but he suddenly gave me that all-out smile that made my legs wobble. "Why don't we make Jess honorary committee chair? Is that okay with you?" he asked. "As I said, it's your idea. We'll do it your way."

I searched for the right thing to say. "What's important is getting the work done," I managed to tell Mrs. Emery. "It doesn't matter to me who heads the committee."

Mrs. Emery said, "I'll call Mrs. Hopkins. She supervises the children's wing of the hospital. I'll tell her what you have in mind. I'm sure she'll be delighted and will give us her full support. Jess, Mark, Scott . . . will you be able to come in after school today so that we can outline the directin we should take?"

I had my mouth open to answer, but Mark said, "We'll be here," and sat down. He reached across

43

the aisle, grabbed my hand, and squeezed it with obvious delight.

What's with Mark? Furious one minute, happy the next, and giving away a plan I'd told him to keep to himself. I struggled to fight back a rush of anger and reminded myself, *I meant what I told Mrs. Emery. It doesn't matter who the committee head is. The plan's going to work out—just what I wanted to help the little kids. That's all that's important, isn't it?*

Sweeping my mind of the raggedy gray lumps of guilt that had made me wish Mark had stayed out of my ideas and plans, I thought, *I should be grateful to Mark. He's just trying to be nice. He's trying to help. And Scott—I guess I'm glad that Scott wants to help, too.*

But something bothered me. Scott had offered to help the instant Mark brought up the idea. I couldn't put my finger on what it was about these two guys, but something seemed odd.

Lori later complained when we met in the cafeteria, "I don't like Mark taking credit for your idea."

I climbed over the bench and opened my brown bag, pulling out a sandwich and some carrot sticks. "It's okay," I told her. "Mark just wanted to get the program going."

"You should be the *real* head of the planning committee," Lori said. "Mrs. Emery wanted you to be."

"What Mark said was right. He's free to help out when he's needed, and I'm not. I wasn't giving in," I told her.

Lori made a face. "Oh, sure. Like you'd have to

44

leave your job and couldn't just call someone to fill in at the children's ward?"

"Lori," I asked, "did you tell Scott what I said about maybe having to quit my job if I got the project going?"

"Of course not," she answered. "I didn't tell him anything about it."

"Then how did he—"

Lori nudged me with a sharp elbow. "Here comes Mark with a cafeteria tray," she said. "And look! There's Scott, too!" She waved to Scott, glowing and smiling like a contestant in a Miss Texas pageant.

As Scott and Mark joined us, I thought I sensed a tension between them, but Scott nodded at Mark, sat down, and pulled out an apple as though they were old friends.

Mark plopped down his tray and asked, "Am I the only one going for cafeteria food? Do you know something I don't know?"

Scott shrugged. "My aunt's not much on making lunches, and I woke up too late to fix one for myself."

As Mark poked at a bowl of macaroni swimming in a bright yellow cheese sauce, Scott added, "My apple looks better and better."

"I've got some Oreos. I'll share with you." Lori beamed at him.

"Thanks," Scott said solemnly, and I wondered if he ever smiled.

"What part of New York are you from?" Scott suddenly asked Mark.

Mark blinked. "What do you mean?"

"It's a simple question, isn't it?" Scott asked. "You've got the accent. I recognize it. So, what part of New York are you from?"

"The Bronx. How about you?"

"Jersey," Scott said.

"Where in Jersey?"

Scott hesitated just a moment. "Galesburg," he said.

"I never heard of it."

"It's there," Scott said, and concentrated on his apple.

As Scott began to demolish the apple, I studied him. *He's lying*, I thought in surprise. *I can see it in his eyes. Why is he lying?*

CHAPTER
five

Late that afternoon, as I hunched over the kitchen table, intent on my homework assignment, a sudden rapping at the back door startled me so much that I jumped straight out of my chair, scattering some of the papers on the floor.

"Jess, open up!" Lori shouted, and then I heard a subtle softening in her voice. "I brought Scott with me."

I unlocked the door and opened it wide. "Hi," I said. "Come on in."

"I'm showing Scott around town," Lori explained as they entered the kitchen. "I told Scott you lived here, so he wanted to come by and say hello."

But Scott stopped short, the door still open, his gaze fixed on Pepper, who had sauntered into the room. "Does he want to go out?" Scott asked, and edged against the wall, clearing plenty of room to the door.

"Don't you like cats?" I asked.

Scott kept his eyes on Pepper. "When we were

47

kids, my younger cousin had a cat, and I hated that cat, but when it died . . . Well, it doesn't matter how it died. It's just that ever since then I don't like to be around cats. They make me uncomfortable."

"You don't have to explain. I know that cats drive some people crazy," I said. "I'll put Pepper outside." I scooped up my squirming, complaining cat, put him on the back step, and closed the door. "Now," I said, "anybody want something to drink?"

"Sure. Thanks," Scott answered. He glanced through the kitchen window toward the Maliks' house. "Lori said Mark lives over there."

"That's right," I answered. As I pulled three cans of Coke out of the refrigerator, Lori bent to pick up some of the papers on the floor.

"What are these?" she asked. "They look like copies of newspaper stories."

"They are. It's my journalism class homework. We have to learn to write headlines for the stories."

Scott picked up the remaining two papers and read aloud, " 'Tucson. The state senate, in discussing financial aid to schools . . .' How about 'Dealing for Dollars'?"

Lori and I groaned, but she said, "Here's one: 'Denver. A mother terrier and four puppies were rescued by a police squad last night when they became trapped in a sewer.' That's an easy headline: 'Big Stink in Police Department.' "

As I laughed, Scott glanced at the top page in

his hands. "Well, how about this? 'Atlanta. A tearful cheerleader was cut from the Gurney Island pep squad for having gained ten pounds.' I'd say, 'Are Women's Rights Measured by the Pound? Ask the Gurney Island Pep Squad Faculty Advisor.' "

"No way," I said, and giggled, not sure if he was joking or not. "Your headline is longer than the story."

"Okay, I'll try another. 'New York,' " Scott read. " 'Twenty-one percent of all shooting victims are under the age of twenty-one, as are twenty-four percent of their killers, according to Police Lieutenant Charles—' " Scott threw the papers down on the table. "Forget it," he said. "The game's getting boring. Let's talk about something else." As he reached for the Coke in my hand, I noticed that his fingers trembled.

Lori took a long slurp of her drink. "We won't stay long. Part of our tour is walking down to the bay."

Scott's attention was drawn to the window again. "Mark just turned the corner on his way home," he said to me. "Why don't both of you go with us?"

Surprised, I answered, "Well . . . I guess I could, except that after our meeting with Mrs. Emery I thought maybe—"

But Scott had already opened the kitchen door and stepped outside. "Hey, Mark!" he yelled.

Through the window I watched Mark loping across the lawn.

"What about the meeting with Mrs. Emery?" Lori asked.

"Didn't Scott tell you?" I shrugged. "We got everything settled, and the project to volunteer at the children's ward is under way. I guess that's all that matters."

"Come on. What happened, Jess? I mean with you and Mark?"

"Nothing," I said. "Mark had some good ideas, and Mrs. Emery thinks he's terrific." Lori raised one eyebrow, and I said, "Okay, I felt like I was on one of those super roller coasters at Astroworld, and it was going too fast, and I couldn't get off."

"Did you want off?"

"Yes. No. No, I didn't. I want a volunteer program, and I want it to succeed. It's just that between Mark and Scott I didn't have a chance to say what I thought about anything. So when Mrs. Emery insisted that I should be head of the committee—"

"She did? Great!"

"Mark was angry, Lori. He tried to hide it, but he couldn't. Maybe he's one of these terribly competitive people. I don't know. But for some reason he wanted to be in charge."

Lori sympathetically put a hand on my arm, but I shook it off. "Scott wanted a big hand in the project, too," I told her. "It surprised me when you two walked in the door, and I was even more surprised when Scott wanted Mark to walk with us."

"If Scott was angry, he's over it now. It was his idea to come and see you. You deserve the credit and to head the volunteers, not Mark or Scott, so just be happy about it."

"Happy about what?" Mark asked as he and Scott walked into the kitchen.

I looked directly into his eyes. "Happy about our meeting with Mrs. Emery. You both had a lot of good ideas, and I know you can make them work."

"Right," Mark said. He didn't look at me. He glanced at the scattered papers on the table. "Homework?" he asked.

"Yes, for journalism class."

His eyes widened. "I didn't know you were on the school paper. I could have saved time and come directly to you." He included Lori and Scott as he added, "Publicity for what we're doing is important. After our meeting with Mrs. Emery I went to the journalism room and talked to Mr. Clark. He took notes and promised there'd be a write-up in next week's school paper." Mark beamed.

He looked like a little kid wanting to be praised. I was confused. Why would two good-looking guys who were new to town get so involved in a volunteer program? I was glad, but surprised. "That's great, Mark," I told him, and his smile grew even broader.

"We're going to walk to the bay," Scott told Mark. "Want to come?"

Mark glanced toward the window. "Walking because you don't have wheels is one thing, but walking for fun when it's so hot? Are you all nuts?"

"We're going to take a path through the woods," Scott said. "Lori tells me it's a little longer but it's shady and a whole lot cooler."

Surprised that Lori would give away our special place, I quickly looked at her. Her lips twisted into a sheepish smile, and she shrugged.

"Okay with me," Mark said.

"I'll leave word for my mom, in case she comes home from work before I get back," I said, and bent to scribble a note, attaching it to the refrigerator with a magnet.

"How about you, Mark?" Lori asked. "You were on your way home when Scott called you over here. Do you need to let anybody know where you are?"

Mark flushed. "No," he snapped, and strode to the door, where he stopped and turned. "Well?" he asked. "Are we going or not?"

"Going," Lori answered. She led the way out the back door, pausing only while I locked the door.

As we came to the corner, Scott reached out and snapped a bloom from Mr. Chamberlin's oleander bush.

With a shriek that made us all jump, a fluffy yellow cat leaped from the shade under the bush and streaked to the safety of the dim front porch.

"Not again!" Mark groaned.

Mr. Chamberlin, his elderly face a puckered, sour-mouthed copy of the cat's, struggled to his feet. "I've been waiting and watching for you!" he shouted, waving his cane at us. "What kind of a stupid, sick, perverted kid are you to get pleasure out of frightening a cat?"

"I—I don't. I mean, I didn't know your cat was in the bushes," Scott answered.

"You're a liar," Mr. Chamberlin snarled. "Get out of here and don't come back! And leave my cat alone!"

"I'm sorry—" Scott began, but he didn't look sorry.

I broke in. "I'm sorry, too, Mr. Chamberlin," I told him. "We didn't hurt Peaches. We just startled her, and we didn't mean to."

His scowl didn't lighten. "What are you stupid kids doing, hanging around here? You ought to be in school."

"It's me, Mr. Chamberlin. Jess Donnally," I said. "I'm one of your neighbors. Second house down. Remember?"

"Of course I remember," Mr. Chamberlin grumbled. "Get away from me. Go home. Just go home." He retreated into the shadows and disappeared.

As we crossed the street, Scott whispered, "Who and what was that?"

"Don't mind him," I said. "He's not a very happy person, so he talks to everybody that way."

Mark bristled. "He called *us* stupid."

"Don't let him get to you. Just feel sorry for him. The only love in his life is his cat."

"Come to think of it, the scowl on his face is like his cat's," Mark said.

Scott nodded. "It's really an ugly cat."

"I don't think so," Lori said. "Persians may have crabby faces, but they also have long, beautiful fur."

"Thus bigger hair balls," Mark said, which made us all laugh.

"He really does love Peaches," I told them. "Peaches doesn't eat cat food. She eats boiled chicken—white meat only—and tuna. Top-quality tuna, right from the can, is her favorite."

Lori took the sprig of oleander from Scott's hand and tossed it into the gutter.

Startled, he asked, "What did you do that for?"

"Oleander is pretty, but it's deadly poisonous," she answered. "You don't even want the juice on your hands."

"Technically, the liquid in a plant is not called juice," Mark began, as Scott rubbed his hands on the seat of his jeans.

Lori laughed. "Hey! School's out for the day. Look—over there's where we enter the woods."

"We came all the way to see this bunch of scraggly trees? It doesn't look like much of a woods," Mark said.

"It isn't," I told him. "It's just a shady way to get to the bay."

"And it's not just a bunch of trees," Lori said defensively. "The woods gets thicker farther back where it joins the piney woods that covers a big part of east Texas."

"Wow! Oakberry's big, famous woods!" Mark teased.

Lori didn't laugh. "It's got real history. Even a cemetery where early settlers are buried, along with a Wild West train robber named Harry Pratt."

Scott perked up. "Where is this cemetery?"

"Nobody knows," I said. "It's probably overgrown with vines and shrubs—if it really exists. It could be a legend."

"Want to go look for it?" Scott asked.

I thought of what I'd promised Mom. "Not now," I answered. "We're going to show you the bay. Okay?"

"Okay," Scott said good-naturedly, and made a turn to the right. We had followed him for only a few minutes when I realized that he was leading us along the path that Lori and I always take.

"You've been here before," I said, but he shook his head.

"Nope. First time."

"You know the way to go."

"I just know that to reach the water we'd have to turn east."

It seemed like a logical answer, and I should have been satisfied. But up ahead lay the rock castle that belonged to Lori and me alone. Into my mind flashed the memory of the last time we'd been there, when I'd told Lori that maybe I should quit my job.

In class Scott had said, "She won't have to quit her job to do it."

I shivered, and Mark took my hand. "Don't tell me you're cold when the temperature is in the high eighties."

"I'm fine," I answered.

Lori giggled. "Don't you know the old superstition? Jess shivered because someone walked over her grave."

I didn't laugh. I couldn't. I was too busy trying to make sense of what I'd just found out. Scott knew what I had said about quitting my job because he'd overheard Lori and me. There was no other answer. Scott had been the one hiding in the woods, spying on us.

CHAPTER
six

I didn't feel like talking until we had reached the bay and were seated on a grassy, hard-packed dirt bank overlooking the flat, blue-gray water. In the distance sailboats skimmed the surface like large white gulls searching for fish, and wavelets splatted the dark soil below our feet in ragged smacks, leaving behind a smear of yellowed foam.

"This is what you wanted to show us?" Mark asked in surprise. "This is where you go to swim?"

"Yuck, no!" Lori said. "Nobody would want to swim here. We drive to Galveston, or sometimes down to Surfside, to go swimming."

"Then why do you come here?" Mark asked.

Lori and I looked at each other. We shared the answer, but I don't think we'd ever actually put it into words.

I was the first to speak up. "Because this is a quiet, peaceful place," I said. "No telephones, no school, no homework, no jobs, no piano teachers, no parents telling us to clean our rooms. We can

57

talk if we want or just sit and watch the sailboats across the bay."

Mark grimaced. "It's not Coney Island."

"Or the Atlantic Ocean," Scott added.

I looked at Scott carefully, hearing the touch of wistfulness in his voice. "Do you miss Galesburg?" I asked him.

Scott looked surprised. "Galesburg? Oh, Galesburg. Yes, sometimes, I guess. It doesn't matter."

"Why did your parents move to Oakberry?" I asked.

"They didn't," Scott answered, without looking at me. He kept his gaze on the distant boats. "I live with my aunt."

I knew I shouldn't pry, but when he didn't add anything else, I asked, "Did your aunt come here to work?"

"She's looking," Scott answered. "She'll come up with something soon."

"Oakberry seems like a strange place to hunt for work. Wouldn't your aunt find more job opportunities in a big city than in a small town?"

Scott just shrugged.

"Where do you and your aunt live?" I asked.

Lori squirmed with embarrassment. "We're not playing twenty questions, Jess," she said.

But Scott turned and for the first time looked directly into my eyes. He didn't blink. His gaze didn't waver. I nervously sucked in my breath.

"My aunt's name is Edna Turner," he said in a monotone, as though his words were rolling out of a tape recorder. "We have an apartment in that big complex over on Dale Street. For reasons I

58

won't go into, I'm living with Edna instead of my parents. Edna and I don't always see things the same way, and I guess you could say we're happier away from each other, so we spend as little time as possible together."

Everyone grew very quiet, and I could feel my face burning. Mom would have scolded me for being rude. Dad would have shaken his head and said, "Jess, you have to stop letting your curiosity run away with you." Lori was probably going to have some well-chosen words to say to me later. And I deserved it.

"I'm sorry," I said. "I sounded like I was being awfully nosy, and I didn't mean to be. I just wanted to know more about you, Scott."

"It's okay," he said quietly.

Mark broke the tension by laughing as he tapped me on the end of my nose. "Is that what they call a nose for news? Is that why you're on the school paper, Jess? Maybe you should get a job on one of those scummy tabloid shows on TV."

Lori grinned, friend to friend. "Or how about being a gossip columnist?" she said.

I went along with the game. "Or maybe write for one of those awful newspapers they sell at the grocery checkout stands? How's this for a lead story? 'Is Scott Alexander all he seems to be, or is he actually a clone, put here on earth by aliens from outer space?'"

Scott looked away. He didn't crack even the smallest of smiles, and I felt worse than before.

"You'd write under an assumed name, I hope," Lori said in a desperate attempt to make us laugh.

While I struggled to think of something funny to answer to ease the tension, Mark scrambled to his feet. "I've had enough communing with nature, and I've got some history and government reading to catch up on. Anybody want to guide me back to civilization?"

We all got up, brushing away clinging leaves and crumbs of dirt, and retraced our steps through the woods. No one said much, and I suffered for having ruined everyone's good mood. I'd really goofed by being so nosy with Scott.

Scott paused as we came to Castle Rock. As though nothing awkward had happened, he said, "I've been thinking about that hidden cemetery Lori told us was somewhere inside the woods. I've decided that it can't be real. It has to be a myth."

"No, it's for real," Lori insisted.

At the same time I said, "Scott! What makes you think that?"

His eyes crinkled at the corners. "Because if the cemetery really existed," he said, "Jess would have found it a long time ago."

Mark and Lori laughed, and I blushed again. "Okay, okay," I told Scott. "I didn't mean to be so nosy. I promise I won't be again."

"Don't make promises you can't keep," Mark said.

Scott peered into the shadow-speckled woods as if he could penetrate the silent darkness. "If the cemetery is there, I'd like to find it."

"The woods near Oakberry covers acres," I explained, "and it gets thicker with vines and underbrush."

"But the cemetery is supposed to be close by, not too far from Oakberry," Lori said.

Scott turned and looked at me. "Have you ever heard of anyone who tried to locate the cemetery? Or anyone who could give directions to where it might be?"

"No," I said. Remembering Mom's words, I added, "Even if it does exist, it wouldn't be much of anything to see . . . vines overgrowing everything, broken headstones . . . that is if there ever were any headstones."

"It could be a piece of history," Scott said.

"We're not exactly positive about Harry Pratt, the train robber," Lori told him. "Mrs. Hickey said that—"

"I don't mean the train robber," Scott interrupted. "I was thinking about the settlers—the people who came this way such a long time ago."

"Speaking of history and makeup reading," Mark began.

But I caught a strange expression on Scott's face. "Let's go looking for the cemetery one of these days," he said. "In the meantime, we can try to get as much information as we can about it so we'll have a better idea of exactly where to look."

Lori appeared to be about as thrilled as if Scott had suggested bungee jumping, but she took a deep breath, smiled brightly, and said, "Okay. Let's."

Mark shrugged and said, "Count me in. Hunting for a cemetery may be the most exciting thing going on in Oakberry."

They all looked at me. For one instant I fought

with my conscience. *After all,* I told myself, *Mom made me promise not to look for the cemetery when I was very young. It's different now. I'm old enough to take care of myself. Besides, I won't be going into the deep part of the woods alone. The others will be with me.* "Why not?" I said. Scott had said "one of these days." That would give me time to talk to Mom about why I *had* to go if the others were going.

THAT EVENING, DURING dinner, I told my parents about the plans for volunteer work at the hospital's children's ward.

Mom put down the bowl of zucchini and studied me. "It's a really fine idea," she said, "but how are you going to fit it into your schedule?"

"I'll work with the children on Tuesdays and Thursdays," I told her.

"But you said that Mrs. Emery appointed you head of the volunteers. That's going to mean a lot of extra work."

"Not too much. We'll all be in on the organization. We'll make a schedule and have a list of subs if someone can't make it. Everybody's eager to help."

"You always complain that you have a hard time getting in your homework," Dad reminded me.

"I know," I admitted. "At first I thought I might have to quit my job, but I realize I don't have to. I've been thinking about the way I do things. Some afternoons I catch the soaps, and I admit I spend a lot of time talking on the phone to Lori. I can cut out television and phone calls and have more time for study."

"Well, hallelujah! We get the phone back!" Dad said, and chomped down on a large bite of meat loaf.

"What about grades?" Mom asked. The wrinkle that had been flickering across her forehead took root and deepened.

"My grades are okay," I told her.

"They could be better," she answered. "Look, Jessie, you're just a little over one and a half years away from graduation, and that means college—*if* your grades are good enough. You've been great about helping to add to your college fund with your part-time job at Bingo's, but I've even thought about your dropping the job just so you could spend more time on schoolwork."

"Mom," I said, "you worry too much. I can handle Bingo's, bring up my grades, and volunteer two afternoons at the children's ward. Honest, I can."

"I wish you'd talked your idea over with us before you took it to Mrs. Emery," Mom said.

"I wanted to," I told her, "but Mark . . . what I mean is, some of the kids heard about it and told Mrs. Emery, and she was excited about the idea, and . . . well, it got started before I realized what was happening."

"I told you, it's a fine idea," Mom said slowly, "and I'm proud of you for coming up with such a generous plan. But I'm not convinced you can handle such a busy schedule. I'm afraid that everything is going to suffer—your studies, your job, even your volunteer hours."

"Mom!" I wailed.

"Why don't we give it more thought before we make any decisions," Dad said. "Jess, please pass the gravy over here."

I picked up the heavy pottery gravy boat and handed it to him. I licked a drop of gravy from my finger and said, "Let me tell you about a little boy named Ricky."

By the time I had finished the story, Mom's wrinkle had vanished, but she said, "I guess you can give the volunteer work a try, but you'll have to prove yourself, Jessie. Your grades can't be just good. They have to be better."

"I think that's fair enough," Dad said. He and Mom looked at me.

"Okay," I said. "I'll prove I can do it."

You've got to, I told myself. *You haven't got a choice.*

True to my promise, I stayed off the phone, ignored the television, and went over and over the assignment in my government textbook, even giving myself a quiz. To my surprise, what I had read not only made sense, it was even kind of interesting.

By the time I went upstairs to bed I felt good about the volunteer program and the part I was going to play in it. Mrs. Emery had said she'd contact Mrs. Hopkins and get her approval for our program, but I didn't want to wait until it was set up to see Ricky. I smiled to myself. I'd pay a visit to the hospital the very next day.

The shades on my windows were rolled up to the top, so before turning on the light I walked to the windows to pull them down. Concerned with nothing but a soft place to sleep, Pepper, who had followed me, leaped onto my bed, claimed his spot, and curled into an already-snoozing ball.

For some reason the streetlight at the corner was out. Only the half-moon's thin light spilled over the landscape outside my windows, softening the mounds of shrubbery and deepening the shadows that clung to the heavy branches of oak and elm. The Maliks' long, flat front lawn was skimmed with silver and decorated with small globs of yellow light that dropped through narrow cracks where the front-room drapes didn't quite meet. Untidy mounds on the curb in front of the Chamberlins' and Maliks' houses meant that their trash had been put out for the next morning's pickup.

Suddenly Mr. Chamberlin's front door opened, gushing a flash of brightness across his yard before it closed.

Peaches's nightly trip outside, I thought. I was about to pull down the nearest window shade when the trunk of the large elm tree at the front of the Maliks' property wavered and thickened.

It can't be the tree that moved, I told myself, *but I haven't seen anyone approach the tree.* Had someone been there, watching and hiding behind the stocky trunk?

In the pale half-light I thought I saw something

65

small streak across the lawn toward the tree and the trash next to it, then vanish into the deep shadows. The tree moved again, then was still.

I squinted, straining to see until my eyes hurt. Could that small shape have been Peaches? No. I didn't think so. Peaches was as antisocial as Mr. Chamberlin. The animal I'd seen must have been a squirrel.

My eyes began to water, but I kept them fixed on the tree. No more strange shapes, no more movement. I ran to Mom and Dad's room, at the front of the house, for a better look at the elm; but in the darkness the tree looked like nothing more than a twisted, bent skeleton with splayed fingers that waggled in the light breeze.

The street was empty. Had someone been there and gone? Or had my eyes been playing tricks on me?

I heard Mom and Dad checking doors and turning out lights, so I walked back to my room, pulled down my shades, and got ready for bed.

For a moment I sat on the edge of my bed, stroking Pepper, wondering if I'd seen something or not.

CHAPTER
seven

The sky had faded to a thin, pale gray, stamped with a transparent, fading moon, when our doorbell jangled sharply and fist-weight blows hammered against the door.

Mom and Dad, staggering from sleep, pulled on robes as they hurried down the stairs. I stopped only long enough to snatch up Pepper before I followed them, my heart thumping.

As Dad opened the door, Mr. Chamberlin, leaning forward on his wobbling cane, stumbled and nearly fell.

"Peaches!" he cried out. "Peaches . . . she's gone. Where's my cat?"

I thought about what I had seen in the darkness, and my heart skipped a couple of beats.

Mom put an arm around Mr. Chamberlin's shoulders and guided him to the nearest living-room chair. "Now, now," she said in a soothing voice, "don't be upset. We'll help you find Peaches."

Mr. Chamberlin's hands trembled as he pressed

them against the round knob on his cane. Thin wisps of white hair stuck out at angles from his face, which was tight with fear. "Peaches went out last night, as she always does. Sometimes she comes back right away. Sometimes she don't. I fell asleep. It's my fault. I should have waited for her. I usually do. But I went to sleep."

"Peaches probably did, too," Mom told him. "Right now she may be curled up in a ball, sound asleep in some cozy spot she found."

"I agree," Dad said heartily. "Mr. Chamberlin, when you're ready, I'll walk you home, and I bet that Peaches will be waiting at the door for you."

I wondered how I could recount what I'd seen and still make sense. "Last night," I said, "I thought I saw Peaches cut across your lawn and run toward the elm tree next door."

They all looked at me, waiting, but what else could I add?

Mom finally broke the silence by asking, "And . . . ?"

"That's it," I said. "It might have been a squirrel, or it might have been Peaches. Mr. Chamberlin opened his front door, then closed it, and all I saw was a small shadow running toward the elm tree. Or maybe she was running toward the trash. Last night the Maliks put their trash near the curb, next to the tree."

"Did you see Peaches leave?" Mom asked.

"No," I said. "I watched for a while, but I didn't see her again." I quickly added, "It might not even have been Peaches. It might have been a squirrel. With the streetlight out, it was awfully dark."

68

Mr. Chamberlin squinted as if he were seeing me for the first time. "You were one of those kids tormenting Peaches yesterday. I recognize you."

As Mom and Dad looked at me with surprise, I said, "We weren't tormenting Peaches, Mr. Chamberlin. I tried to explain to you at the time. One of the boys picked a sprig of oleander, and the branch snapped back. Peaches was probably under the bush, and the noise must have scared her, so she let out a squawk and ran up to your porch."

"It's not the first time that's happened." He snarled and leaned toward me, his face red with anger. "For all I know, you've made off with Peaches. Where is she? What have you done to her?"

Frightened, I took a step back, clutching Pepper tightly, but Dad placed a strong hand on my shoulder, steadying me.

"Mr. Chamberlin," he said soothingly, "Jess and her friends wouldn't hurt your cat. Jess loves cats. See . . . she's holding Pepper, her own cat."

"I didn't say it was *her*. It was that evil boy," Mr. Chamberlin said.

"These kids are not evil."

"That one is. I can tell. There's pure evil in his eyes."

"Who are you talking about?" I asked.

"The one with the evil in his eyes." Mr. Chamberlin nodded to himself and smirked. "I could recognize it."

I backed up against Dad's strong bulk for

reasssurance. "We were on the sidewalk. We weren't close enough for you to see his eyes."

"I know what I saw."

Dad tightened his arm around me, while Mom said, "Mr. Chamberlin, you're tired and upset. I suggest that you go home now. Phil will go with you. As soon as Jessie and I get dressed, we'll look around the neighborhood for your cat."

"Good idea," Dad said. He took Mr. Chamberlin's arm, helped him from the chair, and guided him out the front door.

The moment the door closed behind them I grabbed Mom's shoulders. "Mom! He's crazy!"

Mom nodded. "Don't be disturbed by what he said, Jessie. He lives in a miserable world he created for himself, so just feel sorry for him and help him find his cat."

"Okay," I said, although I was still shaky from Mr. Chamberlin's accusations. "I'll look around the elm tree and see if I can find any sign that Peaches was there last night." Trying to smile, I added, "Maybe she climbed the tree and can't get down."

"Maybe," Mom said.

I ran up the stairs, two at a time, and pulled on jeans and a T-shirt. No matter what I'd told Mom, or what I'd been trying to tell myself, I knew Peaches wasn't stuck in the tree. We'd have heard her yowls all over the neighborhood. And I'd become more and more convinced that the animal I'd seen last night *was* Peaches.

Why hadn't I told them that I'd seen the tree "move"? Why hadn't I admitted that I thought

70

someone had been behind the tree? Because it sounded stupid? Because I hadn't gone outside to find out then and there what was going on?

Mom took off toward the far end of the block, and I made straight for the tree. The sky was a faint, flat blue, already faded with heat. Against it the large elm, its heavy limbs drooping, stood out starkly.

I approached the tree, skirting the stack of boxes and plastic bags containing the Maliks' trash. As waves of the fishy odor of heat-spoiled tuna rose from the top bag, I fought to keep from gagging.

It took a moment for the idea to register. Tuna? Peaches? Had she been drawn by the scent of her favorite meal?

Gingerly I approached the trash bag, but it hadn't been torn open by a ravenous cat. The mound of black plastic remained securely tied shut.

I gasped as another thought—too monstrous to ignore—slid into my mind. "No," I whispered frantically. "No, no, no!"

My curiosity and fear got the better of me; I untied the bag and looked inside.

CHAPTER
eight

The trash had been picked up before Mark and I set off for school, but the remains of the strong, rancid fish odor clung to the air. I didn't tell Mark about Mr. Chamberlin. I couldn't bring myself to recount what Mr. Chamberlin had said.

However, before our first class began, I told Lori everything that had happened—well, everything except about the tree "moving." I still hadn't come to terms with that.

At first Lori was indignant at Mr. Chamberlin's accusations, but she softened when I said, "There was no sign of Peaches anywhere in the neighborhood."

"Poor Mr. Chamberlin," Lori murmured.

"Mom and I looked everywhere."

Lori shivered, wrapping her arms around herself as she said, "I don't know how you had enough courage to look in that trash bag, Jess. What if Peaches had been inside, all stiff and dead?"

"I had to look," I answered. "You don't know

how glad I was that Peaches wasn't there." I slowly shook my head as I thought about it. "There's something weird about that trash bag, though. The can was filled to the top with tuna. Only a small amount was gone. Why would anyone throw away a whole can of tuna?"

"Maybe it got left out of the refrigerator. Maybe it smelled bad when the Maliks opened it. That's not such a mystery."

"I guess you're right," I admitted, but I still felt uncomfortable about it. The first bell rang. I pulled my textbook from my locker, slammed the door, and put Peaches's disappearance out of my mind.

It wasn't until noon that I realized I hadn't taken time to make my lunch, so I had to go through the cafeteria line. By the time I plopped down my tray—with its cardboard pizza, lukewarm applesauce, and runny red Jell-O—next to Lori, she was just finishing telling Scott and Mark what Mr. Chamberlin had said about us.

I climbed over the bench and groaned. "Why did you tell them?" I asked.

Lori looked surprised. "You didn't say not to."

I glanced first at Mark, then at Scott. "Mr. Chamberlin's a bitter, crazy old man. He was just ranting and making up weird stuff because he was upset about his cat. Please don't pay any attention to what he said."

"Which one of us?" Scott asked.

"Which one what?"

73

"Which one did he say was evil?"

"He didn't," I said. "Let's not talk about it. Let's not even think about it."

Mark ignored me and said to Scott, "Maybe we should ask him."

"Oh, don't!" I pleaded. "I told you, he's strange. He'll just go off on a tirade again and won't give you a sensible answer. Calling you evil certainly wasn't sensible."

"But I'm interested," Scott said. "He told you he could recognize the evil. Did he say how?"

"He didn't know what he was saying!" I leaned across the table, gripping the edge. "Please! Forget about it! I don't want to talk about it, now or ever again!"

When neither Scott nor Mark answered, I stood up and reached for my tray.

Mark stood up, too, came around the table, and put an arm around my shoulders. Smiling, he said, "Don't lose it, Jess. If you don't want to talk about that nutty old man, then we won't."

As I sat down on the bench again, Mark's smile stretched into a broad grin. "You might say that Scott and I were just being curious. You'd be curious, too, if somebody said either you or Lori was evil but wouldn't tell you which one. You do understand the word *curious*, don't you?"

I had to smile. "Don't rub it in," I said. "I understand."

Lori asked Mark how much work he had to make up in history and government. As he went into a long explanation, I ate what I could of my lunch. After the bell rang, I carried my tray over to the tray window connected to the kitchen. Scott suddenly appeared beside me.

Leaning close, he spoke in a low voice. "Did you tell Lori *everything* you saw last night?"

I jumped as if I'd been stuck with a fork, and stammered, "W-What do you mean?"

"If the animal you saw had been Peaches, she must have run to someone."

"Sh-She smelled the tuna."

Scott shook his head. "You said the trash bag hadn't been torn open." His eyes searched mine. "Why are you nervous, Jess? What else did you see?"

I took a deep breath, trying to steady myself. Why would Scott be so sure I'd seen something else, unless he *knew* someone had been hiding behind the tree? And the only way he'd know would be if he had been there. "Nothing," I answered, hoping my voice wasn't quavering. "If I saw someone trying to snatch Peaches, don't you think I'd yell or run outside and try to stop him?"

He thought a moment, his eyes never leaving mine. "Yes," he said. "I guess you would."

"What's keeping you?" Lori said as she and Mark joined us. "You're going to be late for class."

As I hurried toward my journalism class, Mark strode up beside me. "You could have told me about the cat and what Mr. Chamberlin said about us this morning, and you didn't," he complained, and the irritation in his voice was unmistakable. "Don't you trust me, Jess?"

"Trust has nothing to do with it," I told him. "Why should I pass along stupid insults? Mr.

75

Chamberlin was raving. He didn't know what he was saying."

Mark didn't answer. We had reached the door of my classroom, and I stopped to face him. His eyes were cold, blank mirrors that frightened me a little, but I was determined to end this problem, which wasn't my fault. "Can't you see?" I asked. "The way you're behaving is exactly why I didn't tell you what he said. Both you and Scott came unglued because Mr. Chamberlin called one of you evil. What does it matter to you what he thinks? I've told you he's a sour old man who thinks the whole world is evil."

Mark took a deep breath. "Take it easy, Jess," he said. "I just asked you a simple question. I don't need a lecture."

"Okay. Maybe I overreacted," I answered. "But first Scott bugged me, then you."

"What did Scott say?" Mark asked.

The bell clanged noisily over our heads. I shouted, "I'm late for class!" and threw open the door. I was feeling a little angry, too. For the moment I'd had enough of Mark.

I SLID INTO the nearest seat just as Mr. Clark finished taking the roll. Mr. Clark wasn't the kind of teacher who gave demerits. He just threw me a scalding, disapproving stare that made me want to repent not only of being late but of every rule I'd ever broken during my entire life.

"Before we get to work on our first issue of the

paper, I'm going to take a couple of days discussing a topic of vital importance to a journalist," Mr. Clark said. He sent one last zap my way before he turned to the board and printed in large letters: A GOOD REPORTER IS PRIMARILY AN INVESTIGATOR.

"Now," he asked, looking especially pleased with himself as he turned to us, "exactly what does that statement mean?"

I was eager to get back into his good graces. My hand shot up. I repeated what he'd taught us the first week of the semester: "Don't just take someone's word for what happened. Check out primary sources. Check facts."

"Good answer, Jess," he said. "Now then. What are primary sources?"

He was still looking at me, so I tried to muddle through, wishing I'd kept my mouth shut in the first place. "Uh, the actual people involved in the story. I mean, like if it's something like . . . um . . . the mayor of Oakberry said about . . . uh, well, maybe a contractor for street repair not being honest in billing the city, then . . . um . . . it's important to get the story directly from the mayor, instead of from somebody else, like his secretary."

"What about the contractor?"

"Who?"

"The man accused of being dishonest. Don't you need to question him as well?"

"Oh, sure. Of course," I said.

"All right," Mr. Clark said. "We have that established, so what other primary sources do you check out?"

77

I thought a long moment. No one else raised a hand, so at least I wasn't alone. Finally I admitted, "I don't know."

"The various offices that contain public records." Mr. Clark smirked as triumphantly as if he'd just won a tennis match.

"Write down the following information," he ordered. "Public libraries. Public libraries have excellent clip files on people, places, news, and social events. Many libraries also have available Criss-Cross City Directories, which give names, street addresses, phone numbers (many of the unlisted ones), spouses' names, names of children, income brackets, whether the residences are houses or apartments, and names of neighbors."

Robin Botts, who likes to sit in the back row and who probably reads nothing more serious than the comics and fashion news, waved a hand and said, "I don't get it. Why would a reporter need to talk to someone's neighbors? All my neighbors could talk about is what's on the soaps."

"Let's use the hypothetical situation Jess gave us. You want to interview the contractor, but when you call his office, he won't return your phone calls. He has an unlisted number, so he isn't in the residence pages of your phone book. So you check him out in the Criss-Cross Directory for Galveston. He's not listed there, so you try Houston's directory, and bingo! You've found a street address for him and a telephone number. You call for an appointment, but you're told he's out of town, so you drive to his address.

"His home is in the kind of neighborhood media people refer to as *posh*. There are no automobiles and no sign of inhabitants around the contractor's house, but next door you see a woman on her knees, planting begonias. What's your next move?"

Robin giggled. "I hope you're not going to tell us to help her plant begonias. Gardening is *terrible* on nail polish."

"You're supposed to ask her questions, Robin," Eric Dodson said.

"Right!" Mr. Clark seemed relieved to be through with Robin. "What kinds of questions would you ask this woman, Eric?"

Eric thought a moment. "This would be easy if she were on the Internet. When are you going to cover computer searches?"

"Computers have their uses, but there are other well-proven, tried-and-true methods for extracting information," Mr. Clark said. He scowled as though Eric had said something obscene.

Eric didn't look as if he'd been put down. He had the pleased, almost smug look of someone who knows more than the teacher. If it had to do with computers, I was pretty sure Eric would be right.

I raised my hand again. "I'd ask the neighbor how well she knew the contractor and his family."

"Good," Mr. Clark answered. "I'm assuming that first you introduced yourself and told her the name of the newspaper you were representing."

"Of course," I said, and felt myself blushing, because I really hadn't thought of that at all.

"I'd compliment her on her garden," Robin

said, and giggled again. "My grandmother loves to garden, and she turns into a marshmallow when people compliment her plants."

"I think the point Robin is attempting to make is that common friendliness is a better approach than charging in officiously with a list of questions."

"Sure. That's it," Robin said.

Mr. Clark lowered his eyebrows and glanced around the classroom. "I hope all of you are taking notes assiduously," he said.

No one asked him what *assiduously* meant. We just began writing like crazy.

"A neighbor," Mr. Clark said, "might tell you if the contractor's family had financial problems. Maybe his wife is a compulsive shopper. Maybe the contractor and his wife take periodic trips to Las Vegas and gamble heavily. Maybe they're having problems with aging parents who need nursing-home care or a son who's been accepted at an expensive university and isn't able to get scholarships or financial aid."

"You mean that talking to the neighbor is one way to find out if the contractor needs a lot of extra cash," Bubba Jones said.

Although Bubba wasn't too swift about some things, I knew he'd understand any problem in which someone needed extra cash. Bubba borrowed money from anyone he could.

"Correct. Let's move on to the civil courts now," Mr. Clark said. "You can find out if any lawsuits have ever been filed against the contractor. If any have been, then you can also discover if he's connected to any other businesses or partnerships.

"Through the criminal courts division you will find records similar to those in the civil court office and also pretrial release forms that everyone who goes through our jail system must fill in, including background, relatives, home addresses, and Social Security numbers.

"And in the County Administration Building—"

"Wait!" Robin cried, and rubbed her hand. "You're going too fast."

Mr. Clark paused for less than a minute before he went on. "You'll find tax rolls and property records. In the same building you'll find Uniform Commercial Code Records, which are filed by people to protect their debts. Their assets, such as jewelry, real estate, and collateral on loans, are on record. Also records concerning marriage and divorce and probate. You can discover if the contractor has inherited through a relative's will.

"You can gain information through voter registration records, and . . ."

Robin stopped, put down her ballpoint pen, and rubbed her hand again. "I don't understand most of this stuff," she said. "What has it got to do with putting out a school newspaper?"

"Writing, editing, and publishing the newspaper are just part of your journalism course," Mr. Clark told her. "By the time the semester is over, you'll learn how to be journalists."

As I glanced over my notes, I felt uneasy. "Aren't our private lives supposed to be secret?" I asked him.

"Very few facts about our lives are secret," Mr. Clark said.

"What if I don't want someone to know my Social Security number?"

"You don't have a choice. You have a job with Bingo's Burgers, Jess. Your employer has your Social Security number in his records. A number of agencies have a record of your Social Security number. These numbers are often used in tracking people. Like someone who has moved to another state to avoid paying debts."

"Isn't anything kept secret?"

"Yes. On the basis of the Fourth Amendment of the Constitution and various legal precedents set down by court rulings, people have certain protections against invasion of privacy. For example, criminal records for juvenile offenders may not be publicized, unless—"

"You can find out practically anything through computers and not take so long," Eric interrupted. "You can access company records, school files—"

"We're talking *legally*, Eric. *Legally*," Mr. Clark said. "The practice of journalism involves ethics, as well as legalities, and—"

The bell rang, stopping Mr. Clark in midsentence. I quickly tucked away my notes, glad that this session was over. Like Robin, I didn't want to know all these things, because I was sure I'd never use them. I just wanted to write stories for the school paper. I wondered where I'd gotten the idea that journalism class would be nothing but fun.

In Algebra II, I had to think so hard it gave me a headache, so I was glad when my last class was finally over and I could head for the children's ward . . . and Ricky.

Mrs. Hopkins greeted me with a beaming smile. "Mrs. Emery told me about your plan, Jess. We're both overjoyed. There's some red tape we'll have to work our way through, but it can be done. Do you think you can get your volunteers together by the beginning of next month?"

"Even sooner," I said. "I don't think I'll have any trouble getting kids to volunteer—especially those in my social problems class, so I'll just have to make a chart and fill in names."

"Make a copy for me, too," she said, "with monthly schedules that we can coordinate."

"I'll have to get a list of possible substitutes, too."

"Don't worry about that part," Mrs. Hopkins said. "Volunteering is not like a salaried job. We aren't dependent on volunteers, so if someone can't show up, there's no problem."

With a rush of relief I thought, *This is going to be easy!* "While I'm here could I play with Ricky?" I asked.

"Certainly," she said. "Ricky's desperate for some attention. Tell Alice—she's the nurse with the gray hair—to show you how to wash up. Then put on one of the green scrub gowns."

I did as she said and walked into the room where cribs were lined up against the wall.

Ricky was just waking from a late nap, so I picked him up and snuggled his warm, sleepy body against my own. Through the nearby window, frosted with golden late sunlight, I saw two bright red maple leaves drop from a nearby branch and spiral slowly to the ground. Peaceful little boy. Peaceful day. I was filled with joy.

But another reflection suddenly joined mine in the window glass.

I whirled to face Scott.

"I didn't know you were coming here," I said.

"I didn't know either, until the last minute," Scott responded. "I saw you leave school and knew from Lori this was where you were headed, so I followed you."

"Why didn't you call out? I would have waited for you to catch up."

"I had things to think about."

"So you followed me? That's creepy," I snapped. I thought about his eyes on me as I walked the eight long blocks to get here, and I enfolded Ricky even more tightly.

Scott frowned. "I didn't know it would bother you, Jess. Sorry."

I was sorry, too. I didn't like being followed, or spied on, or lied to, and I was afraid of what Scott Alexander might think up next.

CHAPTER
nine

I ignored Scott and sat on the floor to play with Ricky. "Up you go," I said as I grasped Ricky's chubby little hands and helped him stand.

"Up," Ricky said, and gurgled happily at me.

"I'm going to look around," Scott said, and ambled out of the room and down the hall.

"You said *up*," I told Ricky. "Good for you! Can you say *Jess?*"

"Up," Ricky said. His diaper-padded bottom dropped to the floor with a plop, and he laughed. "Up," he said again.

"We'll work on the concept later, sweetie pie," I told him, and helped him stand again while I tried to put Scott out of my mind.

Scott wasn't like any of the other guys I knew. Hiding from Lori and me in the woods and secretly following me here to the hospital—why? That was a weird way to behave, and if I'd had a choice, I'd have told Scott to get lost. But I couldn't. Lori liked Scott.

I sighed. There wasn't much I could do about Scott. I couldn't even tell Lori how I felt about him.

"Ricky," I said as I lifted him onto my lap, "I'm going to teach you how to play patty-cake, and we're going to forget all about that guy and hope he doesn't come back here and bug us."

"Who's bugging you?" Mark asked from the doorway. He crossed the room and squatted beside me. "Not me, I hope."

I gave a start. "No, not you. You just surprised me. I didn't expect to see you here. I've had all sorts of surprises today."

"I made an appointment with Mrs. Hopkins, but I'm almost ten minutes early," Mark said.

"Why'd you do that?" I asked.

"Mrs. Emery said she'd talk to her about our volunteer program, but I thought it would help if she talked to the kids who want to help. She should hear our ideas straight from us."

My backbone stiffened. "She's all for the project. You don't need to convince her. Anyhow, shouldn't this be a committee action—including Scott and me?"

"Hey, Jess, I didn't mean to steal any of your glory. I know how busy you are, so I was just trying to help."

I said, "Let's get one thing straight, Mark, I'm not doing this for 'the glory.'"

"But it will look great on your high-school record and on college applications. It should impress anyone who checks up on you."

"I'm not trying to impress anyone. That's not my reason." I kept hugging Ricky, who was content to snuggle against me.

I could tell from the twitch at the corners of Mark's mouth that he didn't believe me.

"You wanted to head this thing," he said. "I could give more time than you in setting it all up and running it smoothly."

My patience was almost gone. "If you remember, I agreed with you when you said you wanted to be in charge," I told him. "But Mrs. Emery insisted—"

"I know, I know. It doesn't matter. It ended up the way you wanted it to, didn't it?"

I could hear anger prowling through Mark's words.

Ricky reached up and patted my face. I forced myself to calm down for his sake. I stroked the soft, fine hair back from his forehead and smiled at him. To Mark I said, "There are children here who need attention. Since you're here today, why don't you ask one of the nurses to find a scrub gown for you and play with one of the children?"

"I'm not interested in playing with kids," Mark said. "I'm not good with diapers or runny noses or kids at all. They're like cats or dogs. They want so much, and what do they give back? I would have been great at keeping records, making assignments, all the executive work."

I stared at him. I was shocked by his words, and I hoped he was saying them just to bug me. "From now on you're my number one assistant," I said.

"You can give yourself any title you want. Call yourself Honorable Grand Dork, or Esteemed Noble Excellency, or whatever will impress people who'll want to see your high-school records! Just don't give me any more grief about this committee!" I shook my head. "I can't believe you don't even like kids. Why'd you get into all this?"

Mark's voice was sorrowful as he said, "You just don't understand. I only want to help you, Jess. You're the only real friend I have here in Oakberry."

"I'm sorry, Mark." I reached out a hand, but Mark let it slide from his arm as he got to his feet. "I didn't mean to blow off steam," I told him.

He looked at his watch. "I'll keep my appointment with Mrs. Hopkins—that is, if I have your permission."

"Mark . . ."

"Jess, you're going to do a great job. I'm glad I'm going to be part of your committee," he said. "Are we friends again?" His smile was warm.

"Of course we're friends," I answered, bewildered because I couldn't understand how quickly he went from anger to sorrow to friendship.

"Great! I'll see you later," he said.

I didn't see Mark again, but half an hour later Mrs. Hopkins came to tell me that the trays from the kitchen were on their way and it was almost time to feed the children.

"I'll help," I offered.

She took Ricky from my arms and said, "Thank you, Jess, but we'd better wait until we have the final word on rules and regulations from the hospital's legal department concerning what volunteers are and are not allowed to do."

As I picked up my backpack, Mrs. Hopkins added, "I'm so pleased with the ideas you and those young men came up with. Providing toys and books for the children will be wonderful."

I looked up in surprise. "Toys and books?"

"Yes," she said. "The polite young man with the dark brown hair mentioned it."

Mark. Why didn't he say something to me? Guiltily I realized that he might have wanted to, but I hadn't given him a chance. If only he hadn't been such a pain.

Mrs. Hopkins smiled knowingly. "I could feel a bit of tension between the two boys. Could it be they're rivals where you're concerned?"

"Oh, no!" I said, blushing in spite of myself. "There's nothing romantic involved. In fact, Scott has been seeing my best friend, and Mark . . . well, we're just next-door neighbors."

"Bad guess on my part," Mrs. Hopkins said, and laughed. "I just thought that since you're a very pretty girl, and they both arrived here when you did, and . . ." She broke off and laughed. "I guess I read too many romance novels."

On my walk home from the hospital I thought about all that Mrs. Hopkins had said. When had she seen the tension between Scott and Mark? I had felt it, but I didn't understand why it existed. Did they both want to make points with university selection committees? Was that all the volunteer work in the children's ward meant?

At first I was disappointed and just a little bit

hurt. Then I told myself, *Mark and Scott's problems are no concern of mine. All that counts is that we give the kids in the children's ward what they need to make them happy.*

I quickened my steps and walked the last three blocks home humming.

As I TURNED the corner, Mrs. Malik was hoisting a heavy bag of groceries from the trunk of their car into her arms. I could see other bags of groceries crowded into the trunk, so I jogged toward her and said, "I'll help you carry those."

"Thanks," she answered. Sweat beads dotted her forehead, which was plastered with sticky, damp strands of hair.

I dropped my backpack on the ground and picked up two bags of groceries, following Mrs. Malik into their house. There was no sign of Mark or Mr. Malik, so we made another trip to the car and carried the rest of the groceries into the kitchen, lining them up on the counter near the refrigerator.

Mrs. Malik leaned against the counter and wiped at her face with the back of one hand. She looked awful. Her skin had a yellow cast, and her eyelids drooped at the outer corners.

"Would you like me to help you with something else?" I asked.

"No. I need something cold to drink." She pulled a pitcher of iced tea from the refrigerator. "Want a glass?" she asked me.

"Yes, thanks," I said. I'd never seen anything

90

like her iced tea pitcher before. The glass formed a green-and-gold parrot, its curved yellow beak the spout. "That's a neat pitcher," I told her.

"Thanks," Mrs. Malik said. "It's a souvenir from a trip to Miami years ago." She put ice into two glasses and handed one to me, but she didn't ask me to sit down. She just leaned against the counter again and noisily gulped down at least half of the tea in her glass.

She held the cold glass to her forehead and sighed with pleasure. "I don't know when I'll ever get used to this heat," she said. "There had to be other, cooler places to live."

"Mark said you and your husband were transferred here."

"Yeah, that's right."

"You have a long drive from the MaxiMart at the Gulfgate Mall."

Her glance was wary. "What are you getting at?"

"I just mean that you look awfully hot. Isn't your car air-conditioned?"

"Sure, but it's broken. Would it hurt anybody if we drove a little newer car?"

Her accent threw me. I had to decipher what she had said before I could completely understand it. "Are you looking for a new car?" I asked.

"Me? Ha! I should be so lucky." She took another long swallow of tea, and it seemed to make her feel better, because she said, "Your mother was kind to send over that cake. I should thank her. I guess I'm not much of a neighbor. I've never been one for visiting back and forth. I'm not sure how to accept all the food that's come over. Somebody brought a pot roast. Somebody from one of the churches in town came over with a peach pie. We don't even know them."

"Just enjoy the food," I said. "They're welcoming you to the neighborhood. It's a custom around here."

"I'd just as soon it wasn't. It makes it hard to keep to yourself."

"It also makes it easier to make friends."

"Friends?" Mrs. Malik lifted the hair at the back of her neck. "No thanks. I like to pick and choose my own friends."

I took another sip of iced tea and put my glass down on the counter. "I'd better get home," I told her. "It's almost time for dinner."

"Thanks for lending me a hand," she said, but she didn't move from where she was standing.

"I was glad to," I said. I walked down the hallway to the front door and let myself out.

As I picked up my backpack, I remembered what I'd thought of Mark's parents the first time I'd met them. I hadn't changed my opinion. They were truly weird.

As I walked into our kitchen, Mom was stirring something in a kettle. I dropped my backpack into the nearest kitchen chair, as usual, and sniffed the air appreciatively. "Yum! Spaghetti," I said.

Mom hugged me. "I went grocery shopping after work. You told me you'd make cheese enchiladas tomorrow, when it's your turn to cook, so I got all the ingredients. Is that all right?"

"It's great," I said. "I haven't made enchiladas for months."

Mom sighed. "I know that nowadays we're only supposed to eat broiled chicken and fish, but then I read that pasta is good for you, and even some red meat . . . except in the paper this morning some doctor said not to eat red meat . . . but I don't really think cheese enchiladas will be that bad for us if we don't eat them too often, do you?"

"Not if you give up coffee, tea, and artificial sweeteners," I said.

"What!" Mom cried.

"Just kidding," I told her. I picked up the lid of the kettle and stirred the sauce. When Mom makes it from scratch, she cooks up tons and we package it for the freezer.

"You'll be eating dinner alone tonight," she said. "Your dad and I will be going to that golf awards dinner at the club."

I pictured Dad grumbling and complaining every time he had to put on his tuxedo. He loves his job as golf pro at the country club but hates the formal dinners he had to attend.

In the distance I heard a high-pitched wail. The second time, it came more clearly. "Peaches! Peaches!"

Mom and I looked at each other. "He's calling his cat," I murmured. "Oh, Mom, I feel sorry for him."

"Poor Mr. Chamberlin. He's terribly upset," Mom said. "He was on his porch calling Peaches a while ago when I drove home, so I stopped by to visit with him after I put the groceries away. He can't believe that Peaches won't come back."

"Mom, what do you think happened to Peaches?" I asked. I couldn't get the picture of the "moving" tree and the streaking cat out of my mind. "Do you think she was picked up by the animal shelter?"

"No," Mom said. "I checked. Maybe Peaches wandered over to a busy street and got hit by a car. I can't imagine what else could have happened to her. Surely no one would want to steal an old cat like Peaches."

At that moment Pepper ambled into the room. To his obvious displeasure, I interrupted him in midstretch, swooping him up and hugging him closely. I knew how Mr. Chamberlin must be suffering. I'd have felt the same way if Pepper had suddenly disappeared. I couldn't bear to think about it.

"Mom," I said, changing the conversation to something happier, "you've got to meet Ricky. He's the cutest little boy, with big blue eyes and hair so blond it's almost white. Today he said one word—*up*—and he said it for everything. He's so cute!

"Oh! Are any of my old toys around? Mark got the idea of bringing toys and books to the children's ward. Isn't that great?"

"Yes, it is," Mom said. "Tomorrow I'll look in the garage to see what we've saved." She glanced at my backpack on the table, where I always dropped it. "But right now take out your books and get busy with your homework. You've got half an hour until dinnertime. I'm counting on what you promised about bringing up your grades."

Exasperated, I answered, "Okay, okay. I'm going to." I wondered why Mom couldn't let me do what I'd told her I'd do without forever reminding me.

With Pepper in one arm and my books in the other, I settled into a comfortable chair in the den. After just one longing look at the blank television screen, I opened my English lit book.

WHEN MOM'S SAUCE had simmered long enough, I boiled some spaghetti and cut up greens for a salad. Mom and Dad came in to say goodbye before they left for the country club, and I told them both they looked gorgeous.

"Men aren't gorgeous," Dad complained. He tried to wiggle a finger between his neck and his collar and said, "Doris, this shirt shrank."

"Either lose ten pounds or buy another shirt," Mom told him.

As they kissed me goodbye, Pepper rubbed against my ankles. "I didn't forget you," I told him. I dished cat food into his bowl and watched him munch his way through it with fastidious little cat bites. When the bowl was empty, Pepper made for the back door, and I let him out.

At last I was able to settle down to enjoy my own dinner.

The house was silent, except for the cycling of the air-conditioner in a monotonous on-off hum. It was growing dark, so I turned on the kitchen light, finished my dinner, and put my dirty dishes into the dishwasher.

As I stood at the window I saw Mr. Chamberlin's porch light flip on, and I heard his plaintive call again, "Peaches! Peaches!"

Aching for him, but not knowing how to help him, I groaned and hurried into the den, where I turned on more lights than I really needed. I found a calendar for October, a yardstick, and a sheet of posterboard left over from last year's science project. Laying them on our large coffee table, I began drawing grids with dated squares. Volunteers could sign up for the days they wanted. When I'd finished, I reached for my government book.

Normally by this time I'd either have been on the phone to Lori or would have turned on the television. But I had a new lifestyle now, because of my promise to Mom and Dad. I wouldn't allow myself to think of anything else but homework— not my thoughts about Mark or Scott, not even the fun I'd had with Ricky.

It wasn't until much later, when I gave a happy sigh and tucked my last finished assignment into my notebook, that I realized there was something I *should* have thought about and hadn't. Where was my cat?

Jumping up to let Pepper in when he scratches at the door is so routine, I do it automatically. But tonight Pepper hadn't scratched at the door. I hadn't opened it to let him in.

My heart pounded loudly, and I gasped for air as I threw open the back door.

"Pepper!" I shouted, but Pepper didn't come.

I turned on the outside light, a glaring spotlight on the garage, and searched the edges where the light melted into the darkness. "Pepper!" I cried.

Grabbing Dad's heavy-duty flashlight, I ran outside, hunting through both the front and back yards, stabbing the beam of light into all the darkest corners. "Please, Pepper, come home," I called over and over again. "Please, please, please!"

I walked the length of the block and back, jumping at any sudden crack of a twig or rustle in the grass. Light shone in tidy squares and rectangles inside the houses that lined our block on both sides. I caught laughter from an overloud TV and part of a heated argument from the Snyders across the street. But I saw no sign of Pepper.

Sick and hurting, I made my way home.

The back door stood wide open. In my hurry, had I left it like that?

I locked the door carefully, turned off the kitchen light, and leaned against the wall, my face wet with tears.

"Oh, Pepper, Pepper, where are you?" I murmured.

A figure loomed before me, its whispered words raspy with rage. "Peaches and Pepper—they're gone forever."

CHAPTER
ten

My mouth opened to scream, but nothing came out.

"What's the matter with you?" A voice croaked, as someone poked me with a cane.

"Mr. Chamberlin?"

"That's a stupid question. You ought to know my name by this time."

I took a couple of deep breaths. "What are you doing here?" I blurted out as I turned on the kitchen light.

"I saw you searching for your cat," he said, "so I came to see what happened. Your door was open, and I walked inside. What did you do with your parents?"

"My parents went to a dinner at the country club," I answered.

Mr. Chamberlin gave a snort of contempt. "Your mother said she'd help me, and a fat lot of good she did."

"Now, wait a minute," I answered defensively. "Don't blame Mom for your cat's being lost. She called the animal shelter and searched all over the neighborhood for Peaches. And I did, too."

"Didn't do any good," he muttered stubbornly. He pulled out a kitchen chair and slowly lowered himself into it. "You didn't find him that took the cats."

I sat down opposite him. "What do you mean? Who took the cats?"

His mouth twisted. "That's another stupid question. Don't you think if I knew I'd tell you?"

"But you said someone took them. How do you know that?"

"Stands to reason. First one cat gone, then the other. Cats don't wander off in pairs."

"Maybe the tuna in the trash hadn't been thrown out. Maybe it was used to lure Peaches."

He leaned forward, his face thrust into mine. "Find him," he said. "Find the one who done it."

"Find who?" I asked. "You keep saying *him*. Did you see someone around here, Mr. Chamberlin?"

He slowly settled back, his eyes dull with fading comprehension.

"Who did you see?" I repeated.

Mr. Chamberlin suddenly slumped, as though someone had let go of a string that held him up. Tears ran down his face. "Peaches won't ever come back," he murmured.

I jumped to my feet and brought him the box of tissues that sat on the kitchen ledge, but even though I pushed the box right in front of him, Mr. Chamberlin ignored it. He ignored me, too, lost in his own mournful world.

"Did you see Pepper tonight, Mr. Chamberlin?" I asked, but he didn't answer.

I tried again. "Did you see anyone around our house—anyone who didn't belong here?"

"Evil, evil in his eyes. I know evil. I can see it." He continued to cry.

Poor old man. I snatched up a handful of tissues and pushed them at him. "Come on, Mr. Chamberlin," I said. "I'm going to take you home."

This time I locked the back door as I left.

AFTER I WALKED Mr. Chamberlin safely to his own house, I tested his alarm light to make sure it was working, and then I decided to search every inch of the ground between his home and ours. What was I looking for? I didn't know. Anything out of the ordinary, I guess. But tonight there was no trash and no tuna.

Where had Pepper gone? What had happened to him?

The Maliks' front door opened, and Mark stepped outside. "Jess, is that you?" he called. "What are you doing?"

"I'm looking for Pepper," I said. "Pepper, my cat."

Mark loped down the walk to join me. He glanced in the direction of Mr. Chamberlin's house, then back to me. "Your cat's gone, too? What's going on around here?"

"I don't know," I said.

"Were they valuable cats? Would anyone want to steal them?"

"Peaches was a Persian, but she was an old cat, and Pepper was—is—nothing more than an alley cat."

"Did Pepper like to go wandering?"

"Not often. He's pretty lazy."

"Has he ever disappeared before?"

I sighed. "When he was younger, he got trapped inside someone's toolshed for a whole day and scared me to death, but during the last few years he's been content to stick close to home. Mark, I've had Pepper since I was eight years old. I don't know what I'd do without him."

Without meaning to, I burst into tears.

Mark didn't say anything. He just put his arms around me.

"It hurts," I managed to say as my sobs turned to dry shudders.

"Of course it hurts." Mark gently kissed my forehead, then both eyelids, and I felt as though I were wrapped in a caring, comforting cocoon. Mesmerized, I leaned against him and raised my face for what I thought would be his kiss on my lips, but he said, "I'm going to take you home, Jess. I'll wait with you until your parents come back, if you want me to."

It took a few moments to pull myself back to reality. "I'll be fine by myself," I told him. "But thanks for your help. I'm sorry I dumped all my feelings on you."

Mark smiled. "Hey, what are neighbors for?"

I smiled back. "I thought neighbors were different in the Bronx."

"Neighbors are neighbors everywhere," Mark said. "I have to admit, though, I'd rather be neighbors with you than with Mr. Chamberlin."

"I found him inside my house tonight," I said as we walked to my back door. "I didn't know he was there, and he nearly scared me to death. He said strange things, like 'Peaches and Pepper are gone away forever,' and he talked about 'him that took the cats.'"

"What? Did he say he saw who took them?"

"He said he didn't, and I know he doesn't have any idea of what happened to Peaches. But he has it in his head that someone took the cats away. He talked about evil eyes again. Poor Mr. Chamberlin lives in a world of his own since he lost his family."

I said good-night to Mark, locked the door, and double-checked the front door to make sure it was fastened. I searched each downstairs room carefully, feeling like a little girl who is sure a monster lives under her bed. I had no idea what I was looking for, but I found it when I climbed the stairs and entered my bedroom.

A fishy odor drew me to the wastepaper basket next to my desk. Inside lay an open, nearly full can of tuna.

This was a message. I had no hopes of ever seeing Pepper again.

Numb with horror and fear, I picked up the can, took it downstairs, and wrapped it securely inside a plastic bag to block the smell. In the darkness I walked out to the garage and stuffed the bag down under the trash in the large plastic can. I knew I should tell somebody, but I decided not to. The police wouldn't get serious about a missing cat.

I lingered on the back steps, staring out into the darkness. "Whoever you are, you're sick and you're cruel," I whispered, "but you're not going to get away from me. I'm going to find you and stop you."

CHAPTER
eleven

When Mom and Dad came home around eleven-thirty, I pretended I was asleep. I had too much to think about. I lay staring into the darkness long after my parents had climbed into bed and turned out their lights.

In my mind I had already tucked them in, as though they were loving children to be protected. I didn't want to take any chance that they would restrict what I had to do by trying to protect me. That was why I'd decided not to tell them what had happened.

Step by step, I went over everything I could think about that tied into Pepper and Peaches. I ruled out our longtime neighbors as suspects. They'd been friends for years, and none of them would ever hurt a cat.

Mr. Chamberlin might have been in our house uninvited, but he would no more harm Pepper than he would Peaches, and it would have been difficult for him to climb our flight of stairs.

I couldn't believe it could be Mark or his parents, the new neighbors, and even though Scott hated cats, what reason would he have for hurting the cats? No sane person would do it.

I shuddered, pulling the covers up around my ears. The person who had done this had to be mentally ill.

At the breakfast table I told Mom and Dad that Pepper had disappeared. I could see they were very upset, but they obviously wanted to reassure me.

"Remember the toolshed?" they said almost in unison.

"He's probably trapped somewhere and will show up in a few hours, hungry and complaining," Dad told me.

Mom gulped down her coffee and said, "We'll hunt for Pepper, Jessie. I'll finish getting dressed, and we'll start right now." She paused as she pushed back her chair. "It's odd, isn't it, how Peaches vanished one day, then Pepper the next? That seems like too much of a coincidence. I don't understand it."

Dad frowned and said, "Somewhere I read about stealing animals to sell to laboratories, but surely nothing like that would go on in our community."

"Don't talk like that, Phil!" Mom said, and threw a glance in my direction.

"It's okay," I said. "I thought about it, too."

Mom patted my hand, then squeezed it. "Well, it didn't happen to Pepper. We'll find your cat, Jessie. He's going to be all right."

"Thanks, Mom," I said, because she looked as

miserable as I felt. I couldn't bring myself to tell her about the can of tuna—the clue that Pepper was never coming back.

When Mark came by to walk with me to school, he didn't mention Pepper, and I was glad. I guess we both knew the tears might start again.

But Mark told Lori, who gave me a quick hug. "Remember when Pepper was stuck in somebody's toolshed?" she asked. "I bet he'll come home sometime today."

"I hope so," I said. I had to keep the knowledge about the tuna can to myself.

Scott seemed upset by the news. He tried to hide his feelings, but I could see them, and they puzzled me. "I'm sorry, Jess," he told me, but it wasn't sorrow I saw in his eyes before he looked away. For an instant I thought it was fear.

I managed to get through most of the day by deliberately banishing Pepper from my thoughts and concentrating hard on what was going on in each class. The only bright spot was that when I tacked up my volunteer chart in social problems class, a lot of the kids signed up.

In journalism class Mr. Clark first handed back the papers and then went over the headlines we had written. I'd been given a B plus, and he'd written a note to tell me my third headline was "right on the button." That should have made me feel great, but my brain felt like a big, blank hole. I couldn't feel a thing.

I automatically took notes as Mr. Clark continued with his list of places where we could find public information about people.

It was boring until Robin asked, "Does anyone *really* use all this stuff to find out about people?"

"They do, or I wouldn't be giving it to you," Mr. Clark answered.

"Yeah, well, like, I mean not just for a test, but for real?"

Mr. Clark screwed up his forehead and rubbed his nose. I figured he was trying to keep his patience. Finally he said, "Journalists use these sources to gain information, Robin. So do private investigators."

"Private eyes?" Robin said. "Cool!"

"How about computer checks?" Eric asked. "Isn't it about time to go over all the things we can find out through computers?"

"We'll touch on information we can get through computers," Mr. Clark said, but then he returned to the point that Robin had asked about. "Do you understand the importance of being able to discover information about anyone in order to write an accurate, factual story?"

Robin nodded.

"I'm going to make this an extra-credit assignment," he said. "For your own interest, those of you who want to can pick a well-known person and try some of these sources. See what you can come up with."

Mr. Clark went on—but without me this time, because my mind was shooting off ideas like firecrackers. *Okay, Scott Alexander,* I thought, *I'm going to see exactly how much I can find out about you!*

* * *

AFTER SCHOOL I hung around, talking to some of the kids, until I saw Lori leave with Scott. They were heading for Lori's house. That gave me the chance to follow Mr. Clark's list from the beginning. First I'd talk to Scott's aunt or to their neighbors. I headed toward the Heritage Place Apartments on Dale Street.

The building was a huge, brick-veneered complex that sprawled over an entire block. I opened one of the double doors that led into a small lobby, which was decorated in a muddy brown and yellow beige, and knocked on the door labeled Manager.

An orange-haired woman opened the door. "Yeah?" she asked, without really looking at me, and took a long swallow from a can of diet soda.

"I came to see a friend of mine, but I don't know the apartment number," I said.

"What's the name?"

"His name is Scott Alexander."

She shrugged. "Don't have to look it up. We haven't got any Alexanders registered here."

As she began to close the door, I called, "Wait! Please! Don't you remember a woman renting an apartment for herself and her nephew? It was probably just a couple of weeks ago. Her name is Edna Turner."

For the first time she looked at me. "This Scott Alexander. Is he about your age?"

"Yes," I said. "He's tall and blond. Probably seventeen."

She nodded. "Sure," she said. "I remember the kid, but his aunt's a blank. He brought in the

108

check for the first and last month's payment. He said she was sick or something."

"Her name would be on the lease, wouldn't it?" I asked.

She yawned and burped at the same time. She rubbed the back of one arm across her mouth and frowned. "I'd have to look it up."

"Could you? Please? Please?"

"What's the difference what his aunt's name is, if I give you his apartment number?"

I couldn't think of a single good reason. "It's very important to me," I said, hoping that would be enough.

The woman looked at her watch. "Okay. *Oprah* won't be on for another twenty minutes, and I got nothing much else to do. Come on into the office."

It took only a minute for her to pull out a large bound record book and look up the lease. "Edna Turner is her name, all right," she said, "and I was wrong. They didn't pay by check. It was a money order."

Her lips twisted into a smile. "Kind of like him, do you? Want his phone number? Better look it up under Turner."

"It's not like that," I said.

"Oh, sure," she answered. She drained the last of her soft drink, patted her stomach, and burped. "Sorry," she said, "but a good belch makes me feel better. There's lots of stress on this job."

"Does the lease give any other information? Like where Mrs. Turner and Scott came from?" I asked.

109

"Nope. We don't require references."

I studied the book, trying to read upside down, and thought about some of the things Mr. Clark had told us. "Don't you ask for the names of your tenants' banks? Or where they work? Or Social Security numbers?"

"Why should I tell you all that? What business is it of yours?"

"None, I guess," I admitted. "It's just important for me to know."

"Not in my book," she said, and tucked the large volume into one of her desk drawers.

"You didn't tell me Scott's apartment number," I said.

"Two hundred and ninety-six, Building C," she said. "Go out the glass doors on the far side of the lobby and turn right. Building C is between the swimming pool and the side street. Two ninety-six is on the second floor."

"Thank you," I said, and got up to leave. She didn't have to give me the rest of the information I wanted. I'd been able to read it upside down. The bank listed was the one where Mom worked, and Edna Turner's place of employment was Spradler's Drugstore.

Scott had told us his aunt was looking for work, so maybe her job at Spradler's had just been a temporary one.

The apartment manager didn't move, so I let myself out of the office and closed the door behind me. I followed her directions to Building C. I took a look at the carport and saw an old, dark maroon sedan parked in the space numbered 296. So Scott's aunt was home. Good. I climbed the stairs, walked down the outside, open hallway, and easily found the right apartment.

I knocked, but no one answered. The drapes were drawn across the double window, except for a foot near the bottom where they hung crookedly apart. I was too curious to ignore the crack. I crouched down, cupped my hands around my face to peek inside, then nearly fell back in shock.

The room was bare, except for one old beanbag chair and a small portable television set. A phone lay on the floor next to some dirty plates and a mug. That was it. No other furniture. This was where Scott and his aunt lived?

The door of the apartment next door opened, and an elderly man stepped into the doorway. He tugged at the threadbare sleeves of his faded plaid shirt as he asked, "Are you looking for someone, young lady?"

"Yes, sir," I said. I got to my feet, embarrassed. "I'm a friend of Scott Alexander. I knocked, but no one answered, so I was checking to see if Scott or his aunt was home."

"If they don't answer, it means they're not home. I don't hold with peeking through people's windows."

My face grew warm. "You're right. I shouldn't have. I'm sorry."

He began to close the door, but I couldn't let him. He was next on Mr. Clark's list: Ask a neighbor. I said, "Please don't leave. If you don't mind, I'd like to ask you some questions about Scott and Mrs. Turner."

"Who?"

"The people who live in this apartment. Can you tell me about them?"

"You don't look like a bill collector. What's your reason for wanting to know?"

I smiled. "I'm not a bill collector. I'm in high school, and I'm taking a journalism class. Scott is a friend of mine, so I'm using him as a subject for a homework assignment."

"Homework, huh?" he said, and chuckled. "Okay, what's your question?"

"Has Scott or Mrs. Turner ever told you where they came from? Have they talked at all about why they moved to Oakberry?"

"Who's this Mrs. Turner you keep talking about?"

"Scott's aunt. She lives here with him."

The man pursed his lips as he thought and shook his head. "Never seen her."

"But you must have heard her—maybe the sound of her voice in the next apartment, talking to Scott?"

"Nope."

"But she rented the apartment," I said.

"Makes no difference. I still haven't met the lady."

And neither has the office manager. I was getting more and more puzzled.

"Have you talked to Scott?"

"Oh, sure. Nice boy. We say an occasional

howdy to each other as he's coming and going from school. Once he came by to use my phone before the phone company got around to hookin' his up."

"Do you know who he called?"

He raised one eyebrow. "You're a mighty nosy young lady."

"Journalism assignment." I smiled, but he didn't smile back.

"Whyn't you ask Scott your questions?" he said. "Far as I can see, reporters go right to the source."

"He's pretty modest about himself, so I hoped you could tell me something about him," I said. "Thanks for talking to me."

"Don't mention it."

The suspicion that had narrowed his eyes hadn't left. He stood in his doorway and waited to make sure I was really leaving, so I didn't attempt to talk to other neighbors. I had a better idea anyway. I walked straight to Spradler's Drugstore and up to the nearest clerk.

"Could you tell me, please, which one of the employees is Edna Turner?" I asked.

The woman looked blank. "There's no Edna Turner working here."

"Did she used to work here? Like last week or before that? Even for just a few days."

"No, she didn't," the woman insisted, "and I'd certainly know if we'd hired anyone new—even if it was only for a few hours."

I wasn't surprised. In a way, I'd been expecting her answer. Scott might live with a beanbag chair, a television set, and probably a bed in the back room, but I couldn't imagine a grown woman willing to live in an apartment like that. Who was Edna Turner? And where was she?

I thought about Lori, who was so hooked on Scott, and about how much time they were spending together. I grew frightened. I needed to get more information fast.

"Thank you," I said. I looked around the store and walked to the back where two public telephones hung on the wall. Although Mr. Clark's system of finding out about a person was useful, I needed more information and had no time to go from source to source. I thought of one person who could help me in a hurry. I punched in his telephone number.

"Eric, it's me—Jess Donnally," I said. "I heard what you said in journalism class about how helpful and speedy a computer can be."

"So," Eric said. "What do you want exactly?"

"Eric," I said, "I need you to use a computer to check where someone said he lived, to see if he was telling the truth."

"That's pretty easy," Eric said. "You could begin with the Bureau of Vital Statistics in that particular town or city, and also give his date of birth."

"I don't know where he was born. And I don't know his date of birth."

"Wouldn't it be simple just to ask him?"

"I can't, but I really need to know."

"Jess, would you like me to get this information for you through the Internet?"

"Can you do that? I'd really be grateful."

"I can do almost anything through the Internet. Just tell me the name of the person and the city or town he lived in."

There was no reason to hesitate. Eric wouldn't know Scott or even remember his name if he happened to be in one of his classes. "Scott Alexander," I said. "Galesburg, New Jersey. And he's supposed to have an aunt named Edna Turner."

"Okay," Eric said. "Give me your e-mail address."

"I don't have an e-mail address."

After a shocked silence Eric asked, "You're not online?"

"No, I'm not. I'm calling you from a pay phone," I told him.

"Look, if you're having trouble accessing the Internet, it's a lot easier now going through World Wide Web. I can help you get the software to hook up with America Online or Prodigy or CompuServe."

"Eric," I said, "I don't have a computer."

I waited patiently until he pulled himself together and said, "Well, then, give me your phone number. I'll call you when I find out about Scott Alexander. It shouldn't take long."

"I'll be home in twenty minutes. Call me there, and thanks," I said. Eric had already hung up.

I took time to make one more call. I telephoned the bank.

When a woman answered, I tried to make my voice sound deeper and older and said, "I'd like to verify information given us by an Edna Turner. Does she have an account—either checking or savings—in your bank?"

"One minute, please," the woman said, but it took her less than a minute to come back and tell me that no one named Edna Turner had an account in their bank.

I made it home double-time and dashed through the kitchen door. As I opened the refrigerator to reach for a soft drink, I saw the package of tortillas front and center. *Enchiladas!* I suddenly thought. I had forgotten it was my night to cook dinner.

The phone rang as I was washing my hands. Drying them quickly on a towel, I grabbed for the receiver.

"This Scott Alexander isn't a real person," Eric said without any preliminaries. "You should have told me."

"He *is* real," I insisted.

"Then he's using somebody else's name," Eric said, "because the only Scott Alexander listed in the Galesburg, New Jersey, records, was born on March 31, 1979, and died on May 20, 1979."

I gasped. "A baby!"

Then I had another thought. "Are you sure you spelled Scott's name right?"

"Of course I'm sure," Eric said.

"Then, could your computer have gotten the wrong person?"

"Computers talk to computers, and computers don't make mistakes. People make mistakes," Eric said hostilely.

"I'm sorry, Eric," I said. "What you told me came as a surprise."

"If I find out anything else, I'll let you know," Eric said. "It may take a while, because I'm running out of online time for tonight." He grunted. "Parents grew up in the Dark Ages, and they can't understand what life today is all about!"

"Thanks for helping me," I told him.

Eric said, "No problem," and hung up. He was probably sprinting back to his computer.

I sat down at the table to think. *Who was Scott Alexander? And why was he pretending to be someone he wasn't?* I shivered, suddenly frightened of this person who had stolen the name of a baby who had been born and had died probably in the same year "Scott" had been born.

CHAPTER
twelve

Dad called to say he'd be an hour late for dinner.

"That's okay," I told him. "I'm running late in making the enchiladas. We'll come out even."

When Mom arrived a few minutes later, I was busy grating cheese. "Dad's going to be an hour late, so I'm planning everything to be ready then," I said.

"Fine with me," Mom said.

She glanced around the room and asked softly, "Pepper didn't come back?"

"No," I answered.

"I telephoned the animal shelter. They didn't pick him up."

"Thanks for calling, Mom," I said, and tears came to my eyes.

"It's all right, Jessie," she said, and hugged my shoulders. "I know you feel bad, but if Pepper doesn't come back, we'll get you another cat. Lesley, down at the bank, told me her cat just had kittens . . . cute little black-and-white ones."

I could only shake my head. I didn't want another cat. I wanted Pepper. "Let's talk about something else," I said.

Mom sat down, kicked off her shoes, and rubbed her feet. "How's the studying coming?" she asked.

I stiffened. Much as I love Mom, I hate it when she bugs me. "It's coming, Mom. You don't need to keep bringing it up," I told her.

"I'm only showing an interest," she said. "Your father and I are very proud of you and want you to do your best. Did you accomplish a lot this afternoon?"

"I was working on a journalism project," I told her. "I—I—interviewed some people."

"About what?"

"We're learning about sources of information," I said. "Did you know that just about anybody in the world can find out nearly anything they want about you and Dad?"

Mom nodded wearily, as though it was the last thing in the world she planned to worry about. "I saw a TV show called 'No Secrets in Your Life' last fall." She pushed back her chair, picked up her shoes, and got to her feet. "Where's your backpack?" she asked.

I froze. My backpack! "In my locker at school," I admitted.

"With your books in it? Don't you have homework to do?"

"Yes," I said, "but I had that information search to do. I was thinking so hard about that I forgot my backpack."

"Oh, Jessie," Mom said.

119

"I can make up the work," I insisted.

"Tomorrow," she said.

"Right. Tomorrow."

"That means you come straight home from school and hit the books."

"Sure. I will."

"That also means that you won't be going to the children's ward."

"Mom!" I cried. "Tomorrow's Thursday!"

"I know," she said, "but tomorrow means extra study time." Her voice grew soft as she added, "It's your own fault, Jessie."

There wasn't anything I could say to that, since I didn't want Mom to know about any of my suspicions.

MY ENCHILADA CASSEROLE was in the oven, and I'd just put a mixed green salad into the refrigerator when Lori called.

"Oops!" she said. "I forgot you aren't supposed to talk on the phone. I just want to talk for a second, anyway. I'm not feeling too great—I think I'm coming down with something."

"Oh, no. I hope not," I said. "Listen, there's something I want to ask you. How much do you know about Scott?"

"As much as you do," she said. "He doesn't like to talk about himself. On the way home from school I asked him if he'd like to bring his aunt over for dinner on Sunday. It was really Mom's idea. Scott's been over here a few times and she knows I really like him. I know a lot of girls at school who'd love to go out with him. He hasn't looked at anyone—"

"Lori," I interrupted, "have you ever met his aunt?"

"No," she said, "but I'll tell you all about her when I meet her on Sunday. If I'm not sick, that is."

Hiding my shock, I asked, "You mean Scott said he'd bring her?"

"Not exactly. He said he'd ask her if she'd like to come and let me know."

"Lori," I began, wondering how I could say what I wanted to without its coming out all wrong, "when Scott's with you . . . I mean, like when he was at your house this afternoon . . ."

"Oh, he wasn't at my house," Lori told me. "He just walked with me partway. He wanted to explore the woods."

"Why?"

"That's what I asked him. He's still thinking about that hidden cemetery. He told me it would make a good feature story."

"Feature story? Scott's not taking journalism."

"No, but he said something about some historical magazine."

"Oh, for history class." I thought a moment. "Why didn't he ask you to explore the woods with him?"

"I couldn't, because I had a piano lesson."

I hesitated. "Lori, I've been wondering about Scott and where he—"

Mom came into the kitchen and said, "Dad just drove up, Jessie. Can you cut your call short?"

"I'll call you back, Lori," I told her, and hurried to put dinner on the table.

The phone rang again, and this time Mom answered. Because she's a stickler for all of us eating dinner together in peace and quiet, she said, "Jessie can't come to the phone right now, but I'll tell her to call you back after dinner. What's your number?"

She waited until we were seated, then said, "That was Eric Dodson, Jessie. He said to call him back as soon as you can because he has something important to tell you." She rolled her eyes. "Why is it that every little thing with teenagers is vitally important?"

Dad winked. "School dance coming up, Jess?"

"Nothing like that," I mumbled.

"Eric is Earl Dodson's boy," Dad said. "A real brain. Right?"

Mom took a sip of iced tea. "I remember a few years ago when you had a crush on him, Jessie."

"Look, Eric said he'd call me if . . . It's all part of that journalism investigation stuff," I said. "Could I please be excused to call him back now?"

"After dinner," Mom said. "Whatever he wants to tell you can wait that long. By the way, your enchiladas are delicious. Nobody makes them better than you do."

By the time we finished dinner, Dad polishing off the last helping, I was practically squirming off my chair, I was so eager to call Eric and find out what new information he had. But the doorbell rang.

Mom sighed and said, "Jess, could you get it?"

One more delay. I grumbled to myself all the way to the front door, but when I opened it, I jumped. Standing in front of me was Scott Alexander.

"Hi, Jess," he said. "I hope I'm not disturbing you. Could I talk to you?"

"Well, okay." I gulped. "Want to come in?"

"No," he said, and glanced toward the kitchen, where we could hear Mom and Dad talking. "I'd rather talk to you on the porch steps. Okay?"

I called to my parents, "I'll be on the steps a few minutes." I shut the door and followed him into one of those late-September afterglows.

Stiffly I sat on the top step next to him. "If it's about the children's ward . . ."

"I want to apologize. I realized I upset you yesterday. When I said I was following you, I didn't really mean it the way it sounded. I was about two long blocks behind you and didn't want to yell at you to wait. You were going in the direction of the hospital, and I hadn't been there, so it just made sense for me to take the same route. That's all there was to it."

"I did get a different picture. Being followed made me feel creepy," I said.

"I didn't explain myself very well," Scott replied.

I drew on my courage and said, "Scott, I don't think you've been really honest with us."

He sat up with a start and stared into my eyes. "What makes you think that?" he demanded.

"I don't know if I want to tell you," I answered.

"You admitted you're curious. Did anyone ever

123

tell you that sometimes you can get into trouble by being too curious?" he asked.

I stammered, "A-Are you threatening me?"

I began to get up, but Scott took my hand and pulled me back down beside him. "Wait, Jess. That wasn't a threat. I come out with everything all wrong, don't I?" He sighed and said, "There are things I haven't told anyone here for a good reason. All I can do is ask you to trust me."

"How can I trust you when I know you've lied to me?"

Scott leaned forward, rested his forehead in his hands, and groaned. Then he stood and slowly walked down the porch steps. He turned and said, "So long, Jess. I can't say any more. See you tomorrow."

I returned to the house and called Eric's phone number. He answered on the first ring.

"It's me, Jess," I said.

Eric got right to the point. "This Scott Alexander you asked about—he applied last month for a driver's license and got it."

"That's impossible!" I exclaimed. "You told me the only birth record for a Scott Alexander in Galesburg was a baby who had died soon after birth."

"It's not impossible," Eric said. "The government calls it the Tombstone Theory. It's done all the time."

"What's done? You're losing me."

Eric put on the patient tone he'd use if he was talking to a child. "Sometimes people want fake IDs. Usually for illegal purposes. So they pick a name and birthdate that will show up on hospital records. They write to the city or county department of records, give them the information, and ask for a notarized copy of their birth certificate. Then they take the birth certificate to the Department of Motor Vehicles and apply for a driver's license. They can use their birth certificate and the driver's license—or any other ID, like even a library card—to apply for a Social Security number. They can set up a whole new identity for themselves."

"What kind of people would do this?"

"Criminals, people escaping the law, smugglers of illegal aliens. The smugglers arrange for loads of phony IDs and sell them to the illegals."

"I don't understand how it happens. Doesn't anyone in the department that sends out birth certificates check the records and see that the person has died?"

"No, because the date of death would be registered in a totally different department. Only the date and time of birth would show up on a birth certificate."

"Absurd!" I said.

"There's lots of room for improvement. Cross-referencing, for instance, or proof of ID. But at present all that's needed is to pay the fee."

"Eric," I said, "let's get back to this driver's license. Are you telling me that the person who calls himself Scott Alexander is using this fake name on a driver's license?"

"Exactly. A New Jersey license."

"Wouldn't he have to get a Texas license?"

"You didn't tell me he lives in Texas. He could easily get a Texas license by showing his New Jersey one and passing the written and driving tests. If you want, I can check out the Texas Department of Motor Vehicles. Scott Alexander's photo will be on his license, if that's any help. What's your fax number?"

"We don't have a fax."

Eric's words were spaced apart with incredulity. "You . . . don't . . . have . . . a . . . fax?"

"I don't have a computer or a fax. I'm sorry," I said.

"I can't imagine existing without cyberspace or virtual reality," Eric said sympathetically.

"Virtual reality?" I asked, scrabbling through my mind for what I'd read and heard about it. "I know that cyberspace is all the stuff out there on the Internet, but isn't virtual reality just those make-believe games on the Internet?"

"Don't use the term *make-believe games*," Eric said. "Make-believe is for children. Virtual reality is a self-created form of chosen reality. Therefore it exists."

"Okay," I said. "Whatever works for you." Make-believe, virtual reality—they seemed the same to me, but the last thing I wanted to do was to argue with Eric about his Internet world. "Thanks for the information. I appreciate your help."

"Don't go," Eric said. "I'm not through. I found out something about Edna Turner."

"She doesn't exist either?"

"Oh, she exists, all right, but in a cemetery. An

126

Edna Turner, from Galesburg, New Jersey, died last month. It was in the *Galesburg Gazette*."

"I don't believe it!"

"Jess, it's true. I can prove everything I've told you."

Feeling momentarily dizzy, I leaned against the wall and tried to keep my eyes focused through the lights that seemed to whirl around me. "How did she die?" I asked.

"An overdose of sleeping pills," he answered. "The medical examiner listed her death as suicide."

CHAPTER
thirteen

I needed privacy, so I went upstairs and closed my bedroom door. I called Lori. *Answer, answer, answer!* I begged, as the phone continued to ring.

Finally her mother answered, and I said, "Hi, Mrs. Roberts, it's me—Jess. May I please speak to Lori?"

"Not now," Mrs. Roberts answered. "Lori's come down with a bug of some kind—maybe the flu. She's running a bit of a fever. She's feeling miserable and just fell asleep a few minutes ago."

"I'm sorry," I said. "I hope she's better tomorrow."

"I do, too," Mrs. Roberts said, "but don't count on her going to school. I follow the rule of a full day in bed after a fever's over, but I'll tell her you called, Jess."

I hung up. I was desperate to talk to Lori about what had happened. I couldn't just hide in my room. Pepper wasn't coming back. Lori was sick. Was Ricky going to feel forgotten tomorrow?

I wandered downstairs and met Mom in the hallway. She put a thin book with a blue cover into my hands.

"Hamlet," she said. Do something worthwhile with your time. Read a classic."

"Mom," I complained, "we read *Hamlet* last year."

"It wouldn't hurt to reread Shakespeare."

"I didn't mind *Romeo and Juliet*, but this one I hated. Hamlet spent all his time brooding. He whined and felt so sorry for himself. He was terrible to his friends. He messed up everybody's lives —especially poor Ophelia's—because he was determined to get revenge."

"Is that what Ms. Greer taught you?"

"No. I'm telling you the way I saw it. Ms. Greer said that revenge for his father's death was Hamlet's driving force. She made it seem as though he had no control over the way he felt. I don't think that's the way life works. Hamlet should have made up his own mind about what he wanted to do."

"People react to situations in different ways," Mom said. "This is a play, and Hamlet is a character."

"He sure is. He's a real complainer."

"I mean a *fictional* character."

I giggled. "I know what you mean, Mom. I was just giving you a hard time," I said. "But *Hamlet* doesn't matter now, because I got a B plus in the course, and nobody's going to bother me about him ever again."

Mom sighed and was about to say something, but Dad opened the door and walked into the middle of our conversation.

"It took the town long enough to replace that streetlight," he said. "Broken glass. Some kid probably knocked it out. But those things ought to be taken care of the day they're reported, not three days later."

"Phil," Mom asked, "if the light's replaced, then why bother to get upset about it?"

"Because these local government departments take their own sweet time, and we pay the taxes to—"

"Want some iced tea?" Mom asked. "Come on out in the kitchen. It'll cool you off."

I went back upstairs and shut the door of my room, leaning against it in the darkness. My windows gleamed in the brightness from the streetlight—a contrast with last night and the night before. If it had been this bright, I would have seen . . .

To test my theory, I moved toward the windows. I'd almost reached them when I heard a strange *ping* and *snap* and the streetlight went out.

Someone had thrown a rock and knocked out the light!

I pressed my nose to the windowpane, straining to pierce the darkness. There was just enough thin moonlight for me to make out a shadowy form that came toward me from the corner. It blended so quickly into the dark mass of the elm tree that I blinked, my eyes watering. I wondered if I had really seen it or if the figure had been conjured by my imagination, trying to re-create what I thought I had seen the night Peaches disappeared.

In the darkness I watched and waited until the shadows moved again. My heart began to pound, and for a moment it was hard to breathe. Someone was hiding behind the tree, waiting and watching just as I was.

But what was he watching—the Chamberlin house, the Malik house, or . . . our house?

What was he waiting for?

Who was he?

I had to know. Both our front and back doors were visible to this person. If I went outside, he'd disappear, and I wouldn't learn any more than I already knew. If I telephoned Mark and asked him to investigate, the watcher would see him leave his house.

The answer suddenly came to me. I left my room and leaned over the banister at the head of the stairs. "Dad!" I yelled at the top of my lungs.

"Jess? Is something the matter?" he called from the den.

I could hear his footsteps approaching. When he reached the bottom of the stairs, I said, "Dad, somebody just threw a rock at the streetlight. It's out again."

"What!" Dad bellowed like an angry bull and charged for the front door.

I had barely enough time to reach my window

before Dad had turned on our outside lights and was on the porch looking up and down the street. I had hoped the watcher would run and I'd·see him, but the elm tree—its black trunk and branches highlighted in a glaring bug-yellow— stood unmoving and alone.

Dad grumbled as he came back into the house, shutting off the outside lights after closing the door. I leaned against my bedroom window, disappointed that my scheme hadn't worked.

The dark mass of the trunk of the elm shifted. The watcher was still there.

He kept vigil, and so did I, until the last of the Maliks' lights blinked off. The watcher waited just a short while, then slid away. The wide limbs of the tree blocked part of my view, but I thought I caught sight of him just before he reached the corner and disappeared.

I belly flopped onto the bed, where I tried to calm down and think sensibly and rationally. I still had no idea who the watcher could be, but I had learned one thing. He hadn't been at his post to keep an eye on Mr. Chamberlin or on us. He'd been watching the Maliks.

I knew it was unfair to immediately think of Scott. I was suspicious of Scott simply because of what I had learned about him, but he'd have no reason to hide and keep watch. I turned on my light, pulled down my shades, and got ready for bed. It was late and I was sleepy, but my mind kept churning. What was I going to do?

* * *

GOING TO CLASS without having done your homework is probably the next worst thing to nearly finishing a plate of food before finding something strange and gushy in what's left of it. Unfortunately, not just Mom had something to say to me about improving my study habits. Each of my teachers gave a firm opinion.

Mark and Scott sat with me at lunch. We talked about a schoolwide toy and book collection. I missed Lori! I badly needed her to say "Don't worry, Jess. Everybody's entitled to one mistake. So you forgot your backpack and didn't do your homework. The world isn't going to come to an end."

What I'd found out about Scott bothered me. I tried to act as though everything were normal, but it must not have worked, because I caught Scott studying me, questions in his eyes.

Mark stopped talking about the collection and suddenly changed the subject. "When are we going to get together and hunt for the old cemetery?"

"Scott's already started looking," I told him.

Mark gave Scott a sharp, questioning glance. Scott blinked with surprise.

"No, I haven't," Scott responded.

"Lori told me you were going to explore the woods yesterday," I said.

Scott busily searched the bottom of his Fritos bag for the crumbs. "She got that wrong," he said, and looked up. "Remember, I came by to apologize to you yesterday."

"I remember," I said. But Scott's visit had only

lasted a few minutes. He would have had plenty of time to enter the woods. Scott had asked me to trust him, but that seemed unreasonable when once again I knew he was lying.

During our conversation I noticed Mark looking back and forth from Scott to me as though he were at a tennis match.

"But when are *we* going to hunt for the cemetery?" he asked.

"We have to wait for Lori," I answered, guilty that I was using her illness as an excuse. "Her mom told me Lori has the flu, so we'd better not plan on this weekend."

"I think we should call off the search," Scott said. "From what I've found out, the cemetery is just a rumor. We'd be wasting our time."

"When did you come to that decision?" I asked him.

Scott shrugged.

I should have been glad that Scott was making it easy for me to get out of going far into the woods; I wouldn't be tempted to break my promise to Mom, but I couldn't let the matter alone. "You found out something, didn't you? What did you find out?"

Scott's face darkened as he leaned toward me. "I found out that nobody really believes that cemetery is there, except for a few old ladies who keep telling the story over and over. There are no records of it in the city's archives. Nothing. Okay?"

"Okay," Mark said. "We believe you." He began peeling an orange and talking about what movies were coming out, but I couldn't relax. Scott had told Lori he was going into the woods. Why did he tell me he hadn't? He was the one who had been so eager to explore. Scott knew something we didn't. What?

I was glad when the bell rang.

In journalism class we worked on our stories for the next edition of the school newspaper. Mr. Clark assigned me to write the story about the volunteer program at the hospital's children's ward.

When I finished, he read it and made a couple of marks with his red pencil. He gave the work back and said, "Good first try. Make the corrections I've marked and add the names of the committee members."

"I head the committee, Mr. Clark," I said.

"That doesn't matter. The information belongs in the story."

"But then I feel like I'm bragging."

"You're not bragging," he said. "This feature captures a warm feeling about the kids and how much they need volunteers. You did a good job, Jess. People will want to read this human-interest story. That's what counts."

I got a chance to talk to Eric just after the bell rang for the next class.

"Thanks for finding out the information I needed," I told him.

"No trouble," he said. "Any time you . . ." He straightened and slapped the palm of his hand

135

against his forehead. "I got the rest of what you were looking for, too, but I left it home. And you don't have a fax."

"That's okay," I said. "Please bring it tomorrow."

A question had been bothering me since the night before: *Why was someone watching the Maliks?* If I knew more about *them*, I might discover the reason. "Eric," I asked, "is it a lot of trouble for you to look up more information for me on your computer?"

"No," he answered. "It's easy." He smiled. "It's kind of fun, too. It's like being a private investigator. You know that some of them do ninety percent of their work with computers, don't you?"

Dad had mentioned the Maliks' names: Frank and Eloise. I bent over and wrote the three Maliks' names on a blank sheet of paper in Eric's notebook. "Could you check on these?" I asked. "The same kind of information you did before?"

"Sure," Eric said.

If I'd been asked to get information about someone, I would have wanted to know why, but Eric didn't even ask. I knew I could count on his being silent because answers weren't as important to him as what he could do with his computer.

That afternoon I lugged home every one of my books and immediately got to work. I was interrupted by Eric's telephone call. I was awfully glad he'd called before Mom got home.

Eric started with details. "Everything here

136

checks out—names, birthdates, Social Security numbers, former addresses, records of employment, drivers' licenses, school records, all that stuff. There's still a little bit more to come in. Do you want to write down what I have now, or shall I bring it to you when it's all together?"

I heard Mom's car pull up in the driveway. "I'll get it from you later," I quickly answered. "My mom just got home. Okay?"

"Sure," Eric said.

"Thanks, Eric," I said, and hung up.

Mom smiled as she came in and saw me hard at work. "That's my good girl," she said, and kissed the top of my head.

I winced. I was not anybody's good girl. I was somebody who had goofed and got stuck with two days' homework.

"What's for dinner?" I asked.

"It's your father's turn to cook, so I'm pretty sure we'll have Chinese takeout," Mom answered. She took off her shoes and headed for the den.

MOM HAD GUESSED right, but Chinese takeout was fine with me. Good food and not many dishes to wash.

I worked really hard on my homework. I had read in the newspaper and heard on television about different bills being brought up in the House and Senate, but for the first time I really began to understand how lawmaking worked. Government was really interesting.

Mom startled me by appearing in the doorway. "It's getting late, Jessie," she said. "Are you close to finishing up?"

"I'm finished. I was just doing a little reading ahead." I closed the book and smiled.

"Good for you." Mom beamed. "I'm proud of you."

I cringed. "It's just homework. It's no big deal."

I had done what Mom had told me to do, and now she was making it a major case. I admitted to myself that if she hadn't said anything, I wouldn't have liked that either. Why is it so hard for mothers and daughters to say the right things to each other?

Mom surprised me when she added, "Your plan to volunteer at the children's ward isn't complete yet, so there's no schedule to follow. Tomorrow's Friday, and you'll have most of Saturday and Sunday to do your weekend studying, so if you'd like, you could spend some time with Ricky tomorrow afternoon."

"I could do that," I said, and happily followed Mom upstairs.

I switched off the hall light and entered my bedroom. I closed my bedroom door and quickly crossed to the windows, where I waited, my eyes on the old elm tree.

The watcher was there again. I could feel his presence. I knew I was right when the dark outline of the trunk of the tree shifted slightly and settled back.

He and I waited until the last light in the Malik house snapped off. Then the watcher slipped away, and I pulled down my window shades and got ready for bed.

Who was the watcher? If I told Mom or Dad about him they'd call the police. Maybe that was the right thing to do, but I wasn't sure, because I couldn't shake the suspicion that the watcher was a guy who seemed so nice—at least Lori really liked him. But Scott was a liar. I knew that for sure. I just didn't know *why* he was lying.

I'd sleep on the problem, I decided. But it took a lot of tossing, and squirming, and beating my pillow into shape before sleep finally arrived.

CHAPTER
fourteen

The next day, Friday, I left early for school. I'd decided to avoid Mark, and I even skipped lunch period in the cafeteria.

After school, I walked to the hospital's children's ward, thinking only about Ricky.

Mrs. Hopkins met me at the desk. She took my arm and led me toward the ward. "I can't wait until you see what Mr. Clark brought us," she said.

"Mr. Clark?"

"Your journalism teacher. He's so impressed with this project and with the story you wrote about it, he made a contribution—two sturdy Boston rockers. Now our parents and volunteers can rock the kids." She opened the door and said, "Look!"

A woman cuddling a little girl was seated in one of the rockers. She looked up and smiled at me.

My heart jumped. "Oh! I'll wash and put on a gown. Ricky will love being rocked."

The gleam went out of Mrs. Hopkins's eyes,

and she placed a hand on my arm. "I'm sorry, Jess, I have some bad news, too. Ricky was sent this morning to the specialists at Texas Children's Hospital in Houston, because our cardiologist thought he detected a heart problem."

"Nothing can happen to Ricky! He's just a baby!" A rush of hot tears blurred my vision.

Mrs. Hopkins led me out into the hallway and through the open doorway of an office. She sat next to me on a bench and said, "Ricky will have excellent care. We must be thankful his problem was detected early."

I pulled a tissue from the pocket of my jeans and blew my nose. "I was going to teach Ricky to walk. He deserves that."

"There are other children who need you, too."

"It's still not fair to Ricky."

Her grip on my arm was firm. "Jess," she said, "you can give unbounded love to these children, but you have to remember, your love is a gift. It's not an exchange in which the same amount of love comes back to you. And it doesn't tie the children to you. They come and go from here, some of them healed, some of them not; but they all take with them every scrap of love they can get.

"If you're going to give your time to the children, then give your love, too. Give it generously, no strings attached."

I nodded because I understood what Mrs. Hopkins was telling me. Maybe Ricky would come back, but until then, or even if he didn't, I had work to do.

"On Monday a two-year-old named Rachel arrived here," Mrs. Hopkins told me. "She needs someone to play with or talk to. Who here has time to read a book to her?"

I took a deep breath to steady myself, then managed a smile. "Where is Rachel?" I asked. "We can make good use of that other rocking chair."

IT WAS NEARLY five o'clock when I arrived home. Mom was in the kitchen as I dropped my backpack on the table.

"How did it go at the children's ward?" she asked.

"Fine," I said. I remembered Rachel's solemn stare as I sang to her. She had touched my lips and followed their movement closely. Before I left, I had smiled at Rachel, and in return, the briefest of smiles had flickered over her face like the flash of a lit match, brightening her eyes.

"Was Ricky glad to see you?"

"He wasn't there, Mom."

She paused, one hand on the refrigerator door. "Why not?"

I told Mom what Mrs. Hopkins had said to me. "It hurts," I said. "It's been a strange time, Mom. I've lost Pepper. I've had to deal with all these emotions about things I can't control. They just happen."

For once Mom didn't say a word. She just wrapped me in her arms. Oh, how I needed that hug! There were tears in her eyes, but she impatiently wiped them away and said briskly, "Jess, life must go on, and you can face it. Now, would you mind taking out the trash for tomorrow morning's pickup? We've got to do the humdrum no matter what."

"I don't mind," I answered.

I dumped the assorted wastepaper baskets we had around the house into a large black plastic trash bag, hoisted it to my shoulder, and carried it out to the curb. I had no sooner plopped it down than Mrs. Malik drove up and parked her car in front of the Maliks' house. Mark was with her.

As they climbed out of the car, I said, "Hi."

"Hi, Jess," Mark said, but his mother looked just as frazzled as she had two days before. "I guess your air-conditioner is still out," I told her.

Mrs. Malik nodded. "Problems—they never end, do they?" Her voice was bitter.

She obviously wasn't looking for an answer, because she started up the walk to her house. Without stopping to talk, Mark began to follow her. I didn't blame him, since I'd been avoiding him.

"Mark," I said, surprising myself. "There's something I need to tell you. Someone knocked out the streetlamp twice. Once was last night." I glanced up at the post and at the broken glass that still clung around the socket.

Mrs. Malik stopped and turned, bristling as she asked, "What's that got to do with us? Are you blaming Mark?"

"No!" I said quickly. "I'm not blaming Mark. Whoever broke the lights was probably the one who was watching your house last night and the night before."

Mark looked surprised, but I thought I saw a flash of fear in his mother's eyes.

"I didn't mean to scare you," I said. "I don't know who it was. I didn't get a good look at him, so there's not much I can tell you that will be of any help. But I thought you ought to know."

"I'm glad you told us," Mark said, and laughed. "You didn't scare us, Jess, but if we've got some Peeping Tom hanging around, I might put a scare into him."

They turned and continued up the walk as though they weren't the least bit concerned, but I stood where I was for a few minutes, wondering if I had done the right thing.

That evening some of my friends were going over to Gulfgate to hang out in the mall. I decided not to go. I wanted to be home.

I wanted to know if the watcher returned.

He did.

I WAS AT my post at the bedroom windows when the Maliks turned out their lights. But as I waited for the watcher to silently slip away, something unexpected happened.

The door of the Maliks' house quietly opened, and Mark sprinted down the steps and across the walk toward the elm tree. Dark as it was, I could make out something gripped in his right hand.

The tree gave a single shudder and was still, and I stood frozen, almost unable to breathe. The watcher hadn't glided away and around the corner, or I would have seen him. Mark was going to

144

catch him! I didn't want Mark, who was carrying some weapon, to catch or hurt anyone.

As I leaned against the frame of the window, I saw Mark circle the tree, stop as if he were puzzled, and walk around the trunk again. His dark shape moved to the sidewalk, vanishing and reappearing.

I knew where the watcher was. The shudder that shook the tree had told me. He had climbed the tree and was over Mark's head, hidden in the blackness of the thick, heavy branches.

I could tug up the window sash. I could call out and tell Mark. Or I could be a silent bystander.

Finally Mark went into his house, defeated. A while later, the tree shook again. I saw a human shape drop from it and leap to the sidewalk.

It turned toward me with its face uplifted.

I gasped and stepped back. I had thought I was invisible, but from his tree perch the watcher had seen me. I glanced down at the pale reflected moonlight on my white T-shirt before I searched again for the watcher. In one brief instant he rounded the corner and was gone.

LATE SATURDAY MORNING I finished mopping the kitchen floor. I dumped the water from my bucket on the petunias growing in the shade of the back-porch steps and carried the mop and bucket to the garage.

I could hear Mrs. Malik's voice, as shrill as a grackle's, as she argued, "I don't care! I've had enough!"

145

"Keep it down, Eloise! You want the whole neighborhood to hear you?"

The argument went on, but the sound diminished, and I couldn't make out the words. Feeling like a snoop and knowing that curiosity wasn't a good excuse for listening to private conversations, I hurried back to the house.

I grabbed the broom that lay by the steps and was sweeping them clean when a voice from behind made me jump. I whirled around; Scott was standing on our driveway.

"Jess," he said quietly, "I've got to talk to you."

I motioned for him to come in, but he shook his head.

"I see the floor's wet, and I'd just get it dirty again. I'll only be a minute." He squirmed uncomfortably, staring down at his shoes, before he went on. "I meant what I said about staying out of the woods. There's no ancient cemetery to hunt for."

"That's what you told us at lunch period."

"But you didn't believe me. I could see it in your eyes."

It was my turn to look away, embarrassed. "You weren't telling the truth."

"It is really important that you trust me. I know how curious you are, Jess. I can't reveal any more. All I can say is, please don't go prowling around the woods by yourself."

"That's all you can say? You've asked me to trust you before. Why should I? It didn't mean anything. If something weird is going on, I'm willing to listen."

146

Scott sighed. "I can only tell you what I've told you." He shook his head.

"I have just one simple question. Where were you last night, Scott? And the night before?" I asked him.

"Home," he said. "Where else?"

I tried to penetrate his eyes. "Tell me the truth," I insisted. "Trust me, Scott. Where were you?"

"You ask too many questions, Jess," he answered. He abruptly said, "I was home." Then he turned and walked to the sidewalk.

As I watched him turn the corner in the direction of Dale Street and his apartment, I thought about his warning not to go into the woods. What was in the woods that I shouldn't see?

It was bright daylight. I could take a quick look inside the woods and be home in a short time. It wouldn't exactly be breaking my promise if I didn't go *far* into the woods. I walked into the kitchen and called out, "Mom! Dad! I'll be back in a few minutes!" Then I hurried down the steps and across two streets to the entrance Lori and I always took into the woods.

Shade cut off the sun, puddling the ground under the trees with a soft, speckled blue haze. This time I didn't turn toward the bay. Instead I walked silently over the spongy ground into a darker, more heavily wooded area, cautiously moving from clearing to clearing.

I hadn't gone all that far when I stopped short, startled at the sight of two small mounds. They lay close together, and a large, square floor tile of red

147

clay rested on each. On the surface of each tile something had been written in what looked like black paint. Holding my breath, I forced myself to step closer.

On one tile was written "Peaches" and the date she had disappeared. On the other was printed "Pepper," the date, and the inscription, "Here's a little ghost for you."

I shuddered, my body twitching as though it would never stop.

Hands gripped my shoulders. I jumped. Scott's voice said, "I tried to keep you from seeing these."

I jerked away in horror and whirled to face him. "You followed me again!"

"I knew you'd come."

I took a step backward. "Telling me to stay out of the woods was your way of luring me here?"

Scott shook his head. "I shouldn't have said anything about the woods, but your neighbor Mark Malik forced the point. He wanted to set a date to explore."

"These are graves for Pepper and Peaches. How did you know the graves were here?" I demanded.

"I—I accidentally came across them."

"Do you really expect me to believe that?" I said furiously.

Scott's glance shifted to the pair of graves, and he spoke in a whisper. "This was the way I buried my cousin's cat."

In a panic, I backed away. "You . . . you did this?"

"Jess, I . . ."

Scott raised his eyes to look at me, and in the gathering dusk they seemed dark and fearful. I blocked out whatever he was telling me and turned to run.

Tripping, falling, and staggering to my feet, I rushed from clearing to clearing and fought to keep my sense of direction as I groped through the undergrowth and vines that clung to the trees and hung in curling strands like twisted snakes.

Twice I glanced over my shoulder, terrified that Scott would catch up with me. When I caught a glimpse of his white T-shirt through the undergrowth, I cried out in fear.

The patch of white vanished, and from that moment on there was no sign of Scott. It didn't matter if I could see him or not. I instinctively knew that he was silently following me.

By the time the woods had thinned out and I could see the houses ahead, I was gasping, choking, and gulping in air.

I was vaguely aware that someone was running toward me. He grabbed me and held me tightly, saying over and over again, "Calm down, Jess. Take it easy. You're all right."

"Mark!" I gasped, trying to catch my breath. "Pepper . . . Peaches . . . in the woods."

"You found the graves," he said.

"Yes, you knew?" I was shocked but still so shaken that all I could say was, "I've got to tell Mom and Dad . . . and Mr. Chamberlin."

"And I'll help you," Mark said. "We'll tell Mr. Chamberlin first."

"No, not *first*," I said, almost crying.

I tried to pull away, in the direction of my house, but Mark's grip was firm. "I was just with Mr. Chamberlin. He needs you, Jess."

"He needs me?"

"Yes," Mark said.

He took my hand and led me across the grass and up the steps to Mr. Chamberlin's. The front door was open, so we walked inside.

The living room was dark and chilly, shades drawn against the September heat and the air-conditioning set low—too low. I hugged myself, wrinkling my nose at the horrible, sour smell that clogged the air.

"Is he ill? Did you call the doctor?" I asked.

"A doctor won't help," Mark answered. "Mr. Chamberlin drank some iced tea, and soon afterwards doubled over with cramps."

"What . . . ?" I began, but then I saw the pitcher of iced tea. It rested on the table in the small dining alcove and was in the shape of a green-and-gold glass parrot with a yellow beak. "Mark, I saw that pitcher in your kitchen. You brought the tea to Mr. Chamberlin."

"Yes," Mark said. "You look hot and tired, Jess. I'll pour you a glass of tea, too."

"No, you won't! You've put something into it, haven't you? Mark, what is going on? Why were you with Mr. Chamberlin?"

Frightened, I backed against the wall, my shoulder pressing against the button that would make the outside light flash on and off. It was still daylight, and the light wouldn't be as visible as in the dark, but it was the only thing I could think of to do.

Mark, unaware of what I had done, grabbed my arm and jerked me forward until we were in the dining alcove. There on the floor, in a puddle of stinking vomit, lay Mr. Chamberlin.

CHAPTER
fifteen

I pulled away from Mark and dropped to my knees, feeling Mr. Chamberlin's neck for a pulse.

"He's still alive," I said as I got to my feet. "I'm going to call an ambulance."

"No, you're not," Mark said. "The phone's unplugged."

"You're going to let him die?"

"It's his own fault, Jess. It's not mine."

"What do you mean it's not yours? You poisoned him with . . . what?"

"Oleander. I didn't know it was poisonous until Lori told us. So I guess it's partly her fault, too."

I couldn't believe what I was hearing. "You poisoned him. How can you say it was Mr. Chamberlin's fault . . . and Lori's?"

"He talked about me. He said he saw evil in my eyes. He said he saw me capturing your cat."

"You?" I tried to edge out of the room, but Mark caught my shoulder, gripping it so hard I cried out.

"Mark! Mr. Chamberlin didn't know who he saw! I told you that."

"He would have thought more about it and figured it out. I couldn't take any chances. I'm supposed to have a perfect record, be a model student, a good citizen."

I felt as though I were in the middle of a nightmare. Mark wasn't making sense. "Why did you kill the cats?" I asked.

Mark smiled, which was more chilling than if he'd snarled at me. "I told you, Jess. I have a temper. I don't like being yelled at, and I was angry at your attitude about the children's ward project. The credit, the glory—what good would it do you? It would have meant a lot to me."

"You'd kill for it?"

"Who cares about a couple of stupid cats?"

I thought about the tiles that rested on the graves. I thought about Scott's words, "This is how I buried my cousin's cat."

I tried to stay calm. "Are you the one who buried the cats?"

"Yes." He chuckled. "How did you like their headstones?"

I realized I was breathing in shallow gasps. I wasn't going to let myself hyperventilate and pass out. I forced myself to calm down. As soon as I could breathe evenly, I asked, "Mark, you've killed animals before, haven't you?"

"Only for a good reason."

"Did you bury them the way you buried Pepper and Peaches? Did you make headstones for them?"

"No," he said. "It's too much trouble. But once when I was younger I saw a cat's grave with a headstone on it, and I thought it was a good joke. So this time I copied it." He gave a mock bow. "I did it especially for you, Jess. Now . . . how about that glass of iced tea?"

"No."

"Come on, Jess," Mark coaxed. "Make it easy on both of us. The police will find the remains of oleander on Mr. Chambelin's sink, and we'll all mourn the fact that you had iced tea with a senile old man who brewed oleander in with the tea bags. I might even be the hero who finds your bodies and tries to save your lives by calling an ambulance . . . which arrives too late, of course."

"No!"

But Mark glowed with excitement. "I'll take your place as head of the volunteer committee. I'll be a model citizen. I might go so far as to visit the children's ward once in a while and pat a few little heads, but they better behave. Kids and cats remind me of each other. Now . . . there's a drinking glass, and there's the pitcher of tea. Pour it, Jess."

I was no longer frightened just for myself. Through a red haze my terror became a fireball. Mark was a murderer. He was not going to get near those children!

His grip on my shoulder tightened painfully, but I swung my arm out, knocking over the pitcher. The tea gushed across the table, dripping on the carpet.

154

Furious, Mark yelled and shoved me, and I fell, hitting my head on the bookcase that divided the alcove from the living room. For a moment I couldn't see, and I felt myself slipping sideways, spinning around and around and . . . *No!* I repeated over and over as I fought to regain consciousness. I heard voices, and I opened my eyes. Now Mark had lost interest in me. Instead he faced the open front door.

"You're not going to hurt her," Scott said. "I won't let you."

Mark laughed. "I'm taller and outweigh you by at least fifteen pounds. What makes you think you can take me on?"

"You've made a terrible mistake, Mark. Whatever your plans are, you're not smart enough to carry them out."

"You're wrong about that. No one is smarter or more clever than me. Of course I use my genius in the wrong way. A team of doctors told me I am a sociopath. You didn't know that, did you?"

"I knew."

For a moment Mark's bravado faltered. "You expect me to believe you figured that out? Ha! How could you know?"

"For years I've followed you. Ever since you terrorized my cousin's neighborhood. Ever since you murdered him. . . . He was like a brother to me. Paulie was only a child, and you murdered him."

Mark broke in. "You've got that all wrong. I remember what happened. It was *his* fault, not mine. The jury agreed it was self-defense on my part."

"It doesn't matter that some lawyer was able to make the jury buy your lies. You know, and so do I, what really took place."

"It wasn't my fault," Mark insisted, but Scott went on.

"At first I followed what you were doing through neighborhood gossip. We were aware each time you were arrested, and we dreaded each time you were released on probation. Then, when I was old enough to take the money I'd saved and go off on my own, I made sure I knew where you were. I vowed to myself you'd never go free."

Mark hesitated. "I don't believe you. I helped the FBI. The protected witness program is totally secret."

"I'm here, aren't I?" Scott paused only a few seconds, to let what he had said sink in. "No one suspects a kid in jeans. No one pays any attention to him. The Feds bought you that old Chevy on the same used-car lot in Houston where I bought my Ford. I just followed your aunt and uncle."

Mark took a step to steady himself. His face paled. "If you could follow me, then . . ." He couldn't finish the sentence.

"The people you testified against could be after you, too. And I bet they're not as nice as I am." Scott said. "Which is it going to be—them or me?"

Slowly, silently, I pulled myself upright, hoping Mark wouldn't notice. If Scott could keep Mark talking, maybe I could make it out the back door and run for help. I slid a few inches to my left.

But Mark saw me. Before I had time to react, he whirled to grab my arm, then snatched the parrot pitcher from the table, smashing it. He held aloft the handle with its heavy bottom broken into jagged points of glass.

"Back off!" he warned Scott.

"Mark," I pleaded, "Scott isn't going to hurt you."

"He thinks he is," Mark said. "He came to get revenge."

"No," I said. "He wouldn't." I begged Scott, "Listen to me, please. Revenge isn't the answer. It's never the answer. It just leads to more hurt, to more killing, to more—"

"Shut up!" Mark yelled, and shoved me to the floor. I landed so hard I bit my tongue. I could taste the blood in my mouth.

Through all this Scott hadn't moved. Quietly he said, "I didn't come to get revenge, Jess. I came to make sure Mark didn't ruin any other lives." He glanced at Mr. Chamberlin and shook his head. "I guess I failed. When I saw Mark had killed Peaches, I knew he was still sick."

"Shut up! Shut up! Shut up!" Mark yelled. For a long moment he breathed heavily through his mouth, his eyes on Scott.

"Come with me, Mark," Scott coaxed. "Let's get help for you. Let's call the police."

Suddenly Mark lunged for Scott and slammed him in the side of the head with the broken pitcher.

Scott dropped to the floor and lay without

157

moving. I could see a thin trickle of blood creeping down the side of his face.

"Scott!" I cried, and tried to crawl toward him.

Mark grabbed my arm and jerked me to my feet. Holding the jagged edge of the pitcher toward me, he snapped, "Get up, Jess. Come with me. Don't give me any trouble."

"Where?" I asked, trying to stall for time. *Someone notice that blinking alarm light and come to help! Someone! Please!*

Mark gleamed with the smile Mom had said was charming. "I'm going to satisfy your curiosity, Jess. You wanted to see the ancient cemetery in the woods, didn't you?"

"Scott said it didn't exist."

Mark shook his head sadly. "Poor Scott. He wasn't telling you the truth. He's a liar. I'm not."

"He was trying to protect me."

"He isn't doing a very good job of it, is he?" Mark laughed and stepped over Scott, pulling me with him. "He'll be out until I get back to take care of him."

As we went down the porch steps, Mark moved close to me, the glass shards jammed against my side. I glanced toward my house, but he said, "Your father's at the golf club, and your mother's out shopping. We had a nice neighborly visit before she left, which gave me a chance to tell her you had gone to visit Lori."

I tensed, trying to think. *There are other people around who might hear me if I yell, if I—*

"I can read your thoughts, Jess," Mark said with

a chuckle. "I'll give you just one warning. Don't scream."

Within a few minutes we had passed through our empty neighborhood and plunged into the woods.

"Please," I begged, as I struggled to follow Mark over the uneven ground, lumpy with roots and shrubs and an occasional rock, "please don't go past Pepper's grave. It hurts me to see it, to guess what you did to Pepper."

"I'll be glad to describe every detail to`you," Mark said, but when I began to whimper, the glee left his voice. "I can't understand how people can care so much for a stupid animal."

"That's because you don't know how to care for anything or anyone," I told him.

"That's true," Mark said, as though we were having nothing more than a class discussion. "I've heard about love and read about love, but I've never experienced it. I've never loved anyone."

"Not even your parents?"

"Especially my parents."

"Your aunt and uncle gave up their own lives to come here for you."

"That's their problem, not mine."

Mark yanked me over a fallen tree trunk and steadied me as I stumbled. There, in front of us, were the two small graves. "Cat-size," he said. "Child-size."

I shuddered, and he laughed.

"Pull yourself together, Jess," Mark said. "We're going only a little farther. I want you to see the graves we talked about."

"The settlers? You really found them?"

"I did. There's no way of telling whose graves they were, though. Wooden crosses would have disintegrated long ago. There were a couple of stones with names carved on them, but the small cemetery is a mess—a tangle of vines and weeds and underbrush. One grave has completely fallen in."

He paused and smiled with delight. "Considering my change of plans, the sunken grave is made to order. The perfect final resting place for you. An original settler. A goody-goody from the Old World."

CHAPTER
sixteen

I dug in my heels and said, "I'm not going with you to be killed—are you crazy?"

"Don't call me that. You haven't got a choice." Mark's voice was vicious. He held up the pitcher threateningly.

"I have two choices," I said. "I can give in or I can fight. I'm not going to let you kill me without a fight."

"Look," Mark said, his voice changed now, "this isn't my fault, Jess. It's yours. Don't blame me. Blame yourself."

"Everybody's going to blame you!" I caught a flash of movement behind Mark and thought I heard a twig snap. Was someone coming? I talked more and more loudly, trying to keep Mark's attention on me. "The police are going to blame you! The whole world is going to blame you! *You* are the one with the evil eyes!"

"Stop shouting! No one's going to hear you!"

"I can shout if I want to! If I'm going to die, I'm going to scream as I go."

I twisted, driving my arm toward his thumb and breaking his grip. I jumped to one side just as Scott and Eric leaped into the clearing.

"Stand back!" Mark waved his chunk of broken glass at them.

The two of them stood half-crouched, arms extended, ready to spring.

Mark had a weapon that could kill; Scott and Eric faced him bare-handed.

In a flash I thought of my cat and the children who would be in danger and poor dead Mr. Chamberlin. I stiffened my right hand and brought it down in a hard chop against Mark's bent elbow. He yelled, his hand fell, and he dropped what was left of the pitcher.

Before he could react, with all my might, I socked him in the stomach.

Giddy with success, I waited for him to go *ooof!* and bend double so I could bring my clenched hands up hard under his chin. But Eric and Scott were suddenly on top of him in a wild scramble, and I was shoved out of the way.

I grabbed the pitcher's handle, snatching it up so that no one would roll on it, and when Mark's head rose from the scuffle, I banged it with what was left of the smooth, heavy glass bottom. He went down without a sound.

As soon as Scott and Eric realized the fight was over, they got to their feet.

"You were great, Jess," Eric said in awe.

"We've got to get him to the police," Scott said.

"I'll go," Eric said.

Scott shook his head. "He may come to, and for safety's sake we should stick together. Jess, you and Eric each take one of his hands, and I'll take his feet. We'll carry him out of the woods."

"He's heavy," I said. "He'll be hard to lift. He might bump and scrape along the ground."

Eric gave Mark a disgusted look. "I have no problem with that," he said. "Do you?"

I answered by grabbing Mark's right hand. Slowly, and with great difficulty, we carried him from the woods. We yelled as we neared the edge of the woods, "Help! Someone call the police!"

WE TOLD THE police the entire story while we were waiting for my parents to pick us up.

Scott explained, "Sorry it took so long to get to you, Jess. We had to make sure there was nothing we could do for Mr. Chamberlin."

I turned to Eric. "How'd you get involved?"

"Remember, I told you I'd get that information to you as soon as it all came in. If you only had a fax . . ."

"If I had a fax, you wouldn't have been there to help."

"Good point," Eric said. "Anyhow, I was bringing the material over to your house when I saw that alarm light flashing. I ran to see if whoever lived there was in trouble. I found Scott there rubbing his head. He filled me in on what had happened." Eric thought a moment. "My dad keeps telling me that reality is more interesting than virtual reality. I suppose I'll have to tell him that I concede in this one situation, at least."

"Well, thanks, Eric," I said. "You came off the Internet long enough to save us. Why don't you balance your online hours with people hours?"

Eric actually looked pleased. "People hours may be a possibility. I'll give it some serious thought," he said.

I said to Scott, "I'm glad I heard what you told the police. Some of my questions about you were answered. You didn't even know Edna Turner. You just picked her name out of the newspaper."

Scott stared at me in surprise. "You actually thought that I . . . ?"

"Well, it was pretty confusing," I admitted. "Guess you won't be coming back to Oakberry High." I thought how sad Lori would feel. "When you told the police your real name, you said you graduated from high school two years ago." I changed the subject quickly. "What's it like being a freelance writer? Do you make enough money to support yourself?"

One eyebrow arched as Scott answered me, and I blushed. "Not nearly enough," he said. "That's why I'll be leaving to go on to college as soon as I know that Mark Malik—or Wayne Arthur Randall—will be kept from harming anyone else."

I heard Mom's voice raised over a sudden hubbub out in the hallway. I quickly said, "Lori is going to miss you."

Scott stood. "I'd like to be the one to tell her," he said, and strode from the room.

164

I heard Mom shout, "Why do we have to wait to talk to the detective in charge? I want my daughter . . . now!"

"My parents are really upset," I said to Eric.

He grinned. "No surprise. Mine will be, too. But they kept telling me to get a life. They'll have nothing to complain about."

Eric's grin reminded me of how terrific I had thought he was when I was in seventh grade, and I realized my opinion hadn't changed a bit. "Thanks again, Eric." I put a hand on his arm. "I'd like to learn more about all the things you can find on the Internet. Maybe you'll teach me."

"Glad to." Eric beamed.

"First, could you answer a question that's really bugging me? Why is it that Scott's fake background was easy to detect? And Scott's the good guy. But Mark—or Wayne, the dangerous sociopath—had a perfect background, with nothing left out?"

"Scott took what is called the Tombstone Theory and didn't know it could be broken down so easily. The Feds set up Mark's ID, and they're pros at the job. They don't make mistakes."

I pictured Mark standing over Mr. Chamberlin and smiling. And I saw in my mind the graves of Peaches and Pepper. I shuddered. "Oh, yes, they do," I said. "This time they made a big one."

ABOUT THE AUTHOR

Joan Lowery Nixon has been called the grande dame of young adult mysteries and is the author of more than a hundred books for young readers, including *Murdered, My Sweet; Spirit Seeker;* and *Search for the Shadowman.* She has served as vice-president of the Southwest Chapter of the Mystery Writers of America and is the only four-time winner of the Edgar Allan Poe Best Juvenile Mystery Award. She received that award for *The Kidnapping of Christina Lattimore, The Séance, The Name of the Game Was Murder,* and *The Other Side of Dark,* which also won the California Young Reader Medal.

Joan Lowery Nixon lives in Houston with her husband.